STORY TELLING TWENTY FOUR

I0538159

STORY TELLING HAS ITEMS TO MAKE YOUR DAY
VIA POEMS, FUNNIES AND THINGS TO SAY
WORDS TO MOVE YOU, OTHERS TO PLEASE
THEN THERE ARE THOSE WHO ARE THERE TO TEASE.
THERE ARE LONG ONES, INTERESTING ONES TOO.
SOME ARE MISCHIEVOUS BUT NEVER BLUE.
ALL IN ALL A BOOKLET TO HOLD AND BELIEVE.

https://tinyurl.com/y4eo8vp7

STORY TELLING TWENTY FOUR
A DIFFERENT SLANT ON LIFE

978 1 9160587 6.7

Published by

Percychatteybooks Publisher

© Percy W Chattey 2019

Featuring
Famous Names & Events
of the Past

This month we look at

The Lady with the Lamp

And

The Charleston Trust

As told by Richard Seal

Also contained within are chronicles from the 'Hondon Writers Circle' whose members between meetings write narratives on a given subject, hence we have printed stories with similar headings of -

'The Last Day'

STORY TELLING TWENTY FOUR

*Hello - I have a question!
COMMITTEE: Is it a body that keeps minutes and wastes hours.

As always my gratitude to my lovely wife Jean, friend and soul mate, who has helped with the editing and all rewrites, also listening to all my ramblings whilst putting these articles together.

My appreciation to the following

In no specific order

Derek Cook for the cover

Richard Seal

Sarah Dawkins RN, BSc (Hons) MSc <u>AMC</u>

Trudie Oakley

Allan Holdgate

Caroline Goss

Christopher Wyatt

Janet Menday

Janne Tarika Grandal

Lee Halliday

David Filmer

and Your host ... Meg

My name is Meg, and as in the past I will be your host throughout this creation. But first let me explain the following as it is very important:

The contents and the opinions shown or written here are not necessarily the views of 'Story Telling' or its publisher and are published as articles of interest and amusement only and no offence of any kind religious, racial or political is intended to any person or group of people.

I would also like to add on behalf of Story Telling, in a world where there are so many fake and dishonest stories being bandied around, we cannot guarantee items printed here as being accurate or correct and they should be checked in other ways before acting on them.

All the individual work in Story Telling is published with full authority of the originator. If the reader needs further information concerning one of our 'Story Tellers' then please send an email to percybooks@outlook.com we will pass your request on to them

Let's make a start with these True Words

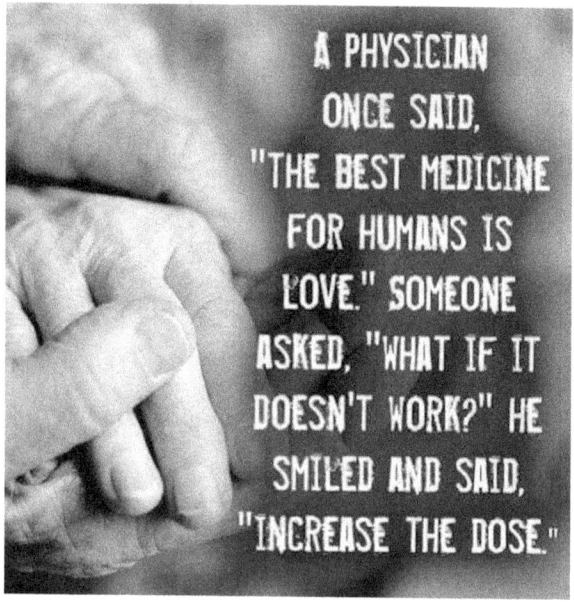

A PHYSICIAN ONCE SAID, "THE BEST MEDICINE FOR HUMANS IS LOVE." SOMEONE ASKED, "WHAT IF IT DOESN'T WORK?" HE SMILED AND SAID, "INCREASE THE DOSE."

**

"To be oneself, simply oneself, is so amazing and utterly unique an experience that it's hard to convince oneself so singular a thing happens to everybody."
Simone de Beauvoir

Penny

Richard Seal

His heart lurches when he hears her voice. Tony stands to meet his childhood crush who is travelling by train for the first time with her six year old daughter and four year old son. Sitting together again, twenty five years on, he nuzzles into lavender scent tingles. Seeing that familiar coy smile, he wonders if Abigail could forget her children for a short while, and run across the fields and climb that stile with him again.

.. Tony quickly reverts to falling down with her onto the cut grass, school field clumps hurled at each other. Her Alice band stolen briefly, he held it aloft with unbridled glee, her arms and long dark hair flailing in laughter. Abigail gave him a penny, slightly sticky, sealing the deal with a little liquorice kiss. It was only the fear of being too girly that held him back from sharing his six pence Curly Wurly.

The last time they had met had been a couple of years later in the park, just before her family had moved away. The swing chain's felt cold on his fingers. Laughing, pushing her too hard, Abigail almost came off with a shriek and promises of sweet revenge. Swapping places, Tony had relished her hilarity as the plastic seat had snapped beneath him.

As her stop approaches, the soft lines of laughter melt back into wedding rings, dark glasses are put on again, and hands touch farewell. He still has her coin though, saved in a match box.

Old Harr'y's Wife'

Caroline Goss

With each turn of the large wheel the paddle steamer chugged through the calm waters of the ebbing tide.....

The early morning mist began to lift and she could just make out the chalky rocks of 'Old Harry' along the Dorset coastline. Until recently there had been another stack of rocks known as 'Old Harry's Wife', but erosion caused her to tumble into the sea. She thought this very ironic, there she was abundantly rich but very alone while Harold her husband to be was waiting at the jetty and he would become the wealthiest man on the Dorset coast.

Tears flowing from her eyes and her heart beating shamelessly she wrapped the large diamond ring in the small silk handkerchief and placed it carefully in the ornate metal box shutting it tight and locking it securely with the small key.

There was now an eerie layer of light between the sea and the mist, and as she pondered this strange hue she tossed the box into the sea followed by the key. She watched the watery circles cascade deliberately out from the fall growing larger until fading into the oblivion of the vast sea. Now it was her turn; she took off her shoes and skirts and placed them neatly on the wooden deck of the boat and jumped ...

..... *With each turn of the large wheel the paddle steamer chugged through the calm waters of the ebbing tide.*

****

Each wave of the sea gently ushered its way up into the cave slowly covering the metal box with the calm waters of the incoming tide.....

Karen struggled to keep awake and as voices grew distant and hollow she drifted into a deep sleep and once again the same dream. The dream mystified her; they started since finding a small silver heart shaped key inside the shell of a slipper limpet a few years ago whilst on holiday at Kimmeridge Bay. She felt the key had a particular significance and kept it as a pendent with the wedding ring of her late husband on a gold link chain around her neck.

Karen was having a wonderful holiday, a far cry from her daily trudge of holding down three jobs; morning cleaning in a large office block, afternoon cleaning in the secondary school and in the evening a bit of bar work just to keep their heads above water. Since her husband's death life had been hard. But this holiday was the holiday of a lifetime that she had worked so hard for, to give her and her children a chance to be in the fresh clean air of the Dorset coast.

Karen woke with a start and in the heat of the day remembering the dream more vividly than ever before; the young woman, beautiful golden hair tied back into cascading curls pinned up with an elegant hair piece, her face as delicate and pale as bone china, and almond shaped blue eyes that drew you into her mind. What was she saying; she's trying to tell me something:

> *My life is as the seas of time,*
> *The love I thought was not mine,*
> *No one could make me wear the ring,*
> *But for you it is the treasure I bring,*
> *Look in the cave of the Old Harry Rock,*
> *For there the treasure you can unlock.*

Karen shook herself from her daydreams on the beach as she heard her son shouting. This was a voice of sudden urgency and Karen immediately got up and raced towards the mouth of the Old Harry Rock cave. "Jack, Jack where are you, come back here at once!"

Karen heard a distant muffle as she ventured further into the cave. The light was beginning to fade as she trod her path carefully through the years of sea worn rocks eroded by pounding waters of the sea.

"Jack, Jack where are you?" her voice echoed hauntingly, she was trying not to sound too anxious but scared of what had become of her son.
The cave began to overwhelm and envelop her with sharp protruding barnacle covered rocks and wet slimy seaweed underfoot. All signs of the outside world now gone, feeling her way pensively her senses heightened.

Suddenly she heard him and with great relief her son in the black shadows of the dripping cave was there in front of her. Karen could just make out Jack as he was clutching onto a metal box; "Mum, mum look what I found!" his excitement far exceeded any concern his mother had for him. She reached out towards him with relief but without any caution of where she was she felt a harsh bang on her head as she slipped and fell.
Had she dreamt that dream again? This time it seemed so real but swirling morning mists and waves of time she saw a paddle steamer and a beautiful woman jump into the water.

"No, no stop, please don't, no!" She was calling out deliriously as she slowly woke up and looked around her; where was she? The paramedics were trying to revive her as she was still calling out. "It's alright Karen", one of the paramedics said in a calm reassuring voice, "You are safe now and we're just off to hospital".

"Jack where are you?", she was beginning to make sense of what happened and saw Jack still clutching onto the metal box before she drifted back to sleep again.

...... *Each wave of the sea gently ushered its way up into the cave as she saw the beautiful woman fade into the waters of time.*

**

IF YOU THINK YOU'RE TOO SMALL TO MAKE A DIFFERENCE YOU HAVEN'T SPENT A NIGHT WITH A MOSQUITO.
— AFRICAN PROVERB

A Day in the Life of a Mountain

Janette Menday

It looks almost forbidding as its sits in inky black gloom waiting for daylight. The early sun lightens the surface of the mountain and a dark mossy green hue emerges from the black. Strangely the furthest point of the mountain appears as a dull indigo.

Darkened folds and crevasses develop as the sun moves across the azure sky, the golden orb and the blue so breathtakingly intense they seem unnatural.

Then, as the sun reaches the horizon, its red glow paints the mountains a lustrous, luminous gold before it returns to its sinister blackness.

**

"Everyone has inside of him a piece of good news. The good news is that you don't know how great you can be! How much you can love! What you can accomplish! And what your potential is!"
— Anne Frank (1929 - 1945)

Westbury '86

Richard Seal

Gary will never forget attending the legendary Westbury Music Festival in 1986 when he had only just turned seventeen. He and his friends Dan and Jon were thrilled at having managed to secure much in-demand tickets, especially as their other classmates had not been so lucky. Gary was a sensible lad, more sensitive than the others, and something of a worrier, while Dan was a happy-go-lucky character, a bundle of energy and a pleasure to be with, and Jon was a loveable rogue who fancied himself as a ladies' man and party animal.

They had been looking forward to their wild weekend away for months, and also excited as a number of top bands of the day were scheduled to be playing. Travelling light, and armed with Gary's dad's aged two-man tent for the three of them to share, the teenagers endured an endless journey in a cramped and stuffy coach from the Midlands all the way down to Cornwall, spending the hours eating packets of crisps and winding each other up about who was most likely to be the champion beer drinker over that long, hot June weekend.

As they strolled with the rest of the crowd towards the entrance to the festival site, Jon spotted a couple of shifty-looking characters at the side of the road, selling alcohol from the back of their van. He insisted that they stop to see if a bargain might be there for the taking.

"Come on lads, we've got no idea what's in this stuff, it could be well dodgy!" Gary felt anxious at the prospect.

"Don't be daft," said Dan, "it'll put hairs on your chest!"

"Or your head down the toilet - it could kill us or make us go blind."

"My brother's made stuff that looks much much worse than this." Jon selected a five litre plastic canister of scrumpy cider. "How about this?"

Dan was on board. "Perfect, that should do the trick to get us started."

"But it's got bits in it!" Gary's protests fell on deaf ears.

Jon clapped him on the shoulder "So has the marmalade on the toast you have for breakfast but you don't object to that. Come on, man!"

Once they had arrived, Gary was overwhelmed by the vastness of the complex and throngs of people milling around, many of whom already looked 'out of it'. The teenagers started swigging from the cider canister even before they had found a place to pitch their tent. Eventually they located a tight spot in the corner of one of the fields, close to some trees.

"This'll do nicely!" exclaimed Dan, "let's have a little drink to celebrate."

"Good idea, perhaps it'll help us to figure out how to put this thing up." Jon gestured towards the tent equipment. "Gary's probably an expert though."

None of them had a clue about how to construct the tent, especially when far from sober, and it took some time and much fumbling with poles, pegs and the instruction book to finally get it up.

"I'm not sure if it's going to survive the night, especially if there's a lot of wind," said Gary.

"We'll have passed out by then and won't notice," Jon replied, "there's nothing to worry about."

"I agree," added Dan, "Anyway, there shouldn't be too much wind inside if we limit the number of burgers and hot dogs. Speaking of which, let's find something to eat."

"I hope we can remember how to find our way back here later."

"Stop fretting, Gary, I've got a great sense of direction." Jon put an arm around his friend. "I'll lead you home safely then Dan will tuck you in for the night."

"That's right, with a bedtime story, a hot water bottle and a cup of cocoa."

"I look forward to it. You'll need to drink some of that too, it looks like all the cider will be gone by then!"

They spent the next few hours visiting the stages, listening to a few songs by each band, eating junk food and steadily emptying their canister. Gary drank the least, reverting to a bottle of water after a while, whereas Jon hit the cider hardest and expressed his disappointment in slurred tones when there was no more left.

"We should get some more, the evening's hardly started ... " The words were indistinct and he was unsteady on his feet.

"Don't worry, the party will get going again tomorrow." To Gary's relief, Dan was on his side. He looked pretty drunk himself, but fortunately he was not at Jon's level. "Can you remember where the tent is?"

"Sure, of course I can."

Jon took a few wavering steps before changing direction twice then falling over flat on his face. The other two had to prop him up as they began the lengthy process of finding their location in the darkness. Each of the fields looked the same, and it was difficult to remember exactly what their tent looked like. Eventually they got back, by which time Gary felt almost completely sober. This was more than could be said for the 'party animal'.

"What are we going to do about Jon?" Gary was worried about the state of his friend.

"He'll be alright after a good sleep, don't worry." Dan looked on the verge of dozing off himself, "Hopefully he won't be sick again. That family wasn't impressed when he threw up right outside their tent were they?"

"He might do it in here!"

"He's looking a bit green, isn't he? We could leave his head outside the tent flap just in case, the fresh air will probably do him some good." Gary felt doubtful about the idea, but he reluctantly agreed. They placed their friend half out of the tent.

"We need to keep an eye on him during the night, make sure he's alright."

Dan fell asleep immediately, but Gary lay awake, thinking about Jon, listening to the strengthening wind and wondering if the tent would stay up throughout the night. His headache was worsening and he felt a bit cold in the sleeping bag.

Gary suddenly heard voices outside. "Hey, what's going on with this guy? He doesn't look so good."

"Too much partying, I suppose. It's par for the course around here of course."

Two faces appeared at the half-open flap, giving Gary a shock. "Hello? Can I help you with something?"

"Yes, mate, you can tell us what you're doing here in our space, in our tent?" The first man's voice sounded menacing through his heavy black beard.

"What do you mean?" Gary felt afraid. Dan was no help, he did not even stir with the intrusion, and continued snoring heavily.

"We've been coming to this festival every year since the mid seventies, and we always stay in this spot. I think it's time you left."

"Leave? Where are we supposed to go?"

The second man, who was disconcertingly wearing sunglasses in the darkness, leaned further through the flap. He had a quieter voice than his friend, but it still contained cold steel. "Look, we are not unreasonable people. You've got ten minutes to get your stuff together and be on your way. Otherwise we will take action."

Gary lay in stunned silence, scared by the exchange. He could not rouse Dan sufficiently to engage in any kind of meaningful conversation, while Jon looked dead to the world. He found himself at a loss at what to do ...

That Saturday was a scorcher, the sun had made its mind up about that from the moment it appeared that morning. Gary was glad that he did not have a terrible hangover when he awoke, although his tongue felt rough and his mouth was very dry. Dan was emitting low groans and stroking his forehead gingerly.

"Did you stamp on my head during the night by any chance, Gary? I've got chimpanzees juggling knives in here!"

"I'm glad you're still in one piece." Gary suddenly remembered the strange threats from the previous night. "What did you make of those two guys who visited us last night?"

"Which guys? I don't remember very much after we started on the cider to be honest, did we stagger back holding Jon up?"

"Yes, that's right." His smile turned to a frown when he noticed that the tent flap was fully open. "Where is he, anyway?"

"Perhaps he's gone to get some more booze - hair of the dog."

"I hope he's okay, he looked awful last night. Let's have a look for him." Gary felt worried.

"I hope he hasn't visited one of the toilet blocks, although that would probably sober him up."

The two ventured out into the sunshine, blinking like creatures emerging from an underground lair. They could find no sign of their friend in the vicinity, and their bleary-eyed neighbours claimed not to have seen the teenager. After searching their field for nearly an hour, they split up to cover the surrounding ones, to no avail. Neither of them wanted to voice their concerns to the other as they walked down to the main part of the site. They ate hamburgers in the hot sun in near silence, while bands were performing nearby.

Gary was in no mood to focus on the music and suggested that the two of them explore separately for a couple of hours then meet back at the same fast-food stall.

Dan tried to cheer his friend up. "I'll probably find him dozing in the cinema tent. Either that or he's hooked up with a troupe of vegetarian teetotallers. Then again, he could have found the light and be preaching to some aged frazzled hippies in the furthest flung corner of the site." Gary grinned, Dan could always be relied on to raise his spirits.

As the friends separated, Gary found himself wandering through a cacophony of sounds around a myriad of stalls, beer tents and groups of people lounging around in the process of turning white skin to red. He kept his eyes peeled for Jon, but knew that the chances of seeing him were slim. He did see a couple of familiar faces walking in his direction though.

The bearded man spoke first "Well, fancy seeing you again. Did you sleep well?"

"Not particularly - thanks to you." Gary stared at him then turned his attention to the other man, who spoke in that distinctive quiet voice.

"You didn't leave when we asked you to last night, did you? I told you there would be a price to pay."

Gary's blood ran cold. "Where's Jon? What have you done to him?"

The bearded man interjected. "I would just worry about myself, if I were you. Have you vacated our tent yet?"

"No, now look here, you're making a big mistake."

The men exchanged glances then started walking away. "The mistake is all yours, mate, we will see you later." Gary felt helpless as he watched them disappear.

After two hours of fruitless searching, Gary found his way back to the burger stall. It was not unusual for Dan to be late, but after waiting for over an hour he started to fear the worst. Enthusiastic though he would have been in other circumstances, he could not bring himself to accept an offer from a group of girls to join them for a few drinks and a game of cards. He continued to look for his friends until the light started to fade.

As Gary despondently made his way back to the tent, he sensed that it was going to be a long, strange night. After getting slightly lost a couple of times, he finally arrived. However, he had not anticipated that strangers would have moved in. He lifted the flap to find the bearded guy and his friend, surrounded by a pile of empty beer cans.

"Well, what do you want?" said the man in the sunglasses.

"What do you think you're doing?"

"We are in our tent, isn't it obvious? You can leave now."

"Where are my friends?"

"How should we know?" The bearded man, as ever, sounded more threatening. "Why don't you go and look for them and leave us alone?"

"This is our tent, our sleeping bags."

"I don't think so. We told you last night and I'm in no mood to tell you again. This is our spot, and always has been. Now I'm warning you - don't come back here again!"

Gary retreated from the tent in shock. There was no one around, no witnesses to the aggressive exchange, he had no one to turn to. In despair he walked over to the cluster of trees at the edge of the field and sat on a stump, head in his hands. After a few minutes he was aware of a low moaning sound. Peering into the darkness, he saw a figure slumped on the ground. He appeared to be tied to one of the trees.

"Hello there, are you okay?"

"Gary, mate, is that you? Can you give me a hand here?"

He was taken aback by finding Jon, and quickly loosened the ropes. "What happened to you, how do you feel?"

"I've felt better! I came around a little while ago and found myself in here. I think I could have got free earlier, but I've been suffering from the hangover from hell."

He hugged his bedraggled friend. "It's really good to see you. We can't go back to the tent, and Dan is missing too. It's a long story. Shall we go for a coffee or something?"

"That sounds like a good idea. I'm starving too."

As they returned to the main part of the site, instinct told Gary to head back to where he had last seen Dan. To his immense relief, the teenager was sitting nearby. He had a black eye and looked rather sheepish.

"Hi guys, sorry I'm late ..."

The three friends sat and ate together, listening to Dan's story. While searching for Jon hours earlier he had encountered the charmless tent squatters. They had manhandled him out of view of the crowds, then the bearded guy had punched him in the face, while the other one hit him over the head with something.

"The next thing I knew I woke up slouched behind a toilet block. Not the nicest place to have a lie in." He rubbed his face. "My watch has gone, I lost all track of time so thought it would be best to come back here. Some girls kindly kept me company for a while and shared their beer with me, so I haven't been too bored."

"Well, we're all together again now, thank goodness. Let's go back to the tent and get changed." Jon seemed more or less back to his usual self .. "Then we can look for your girlfriends, Dan."

Gary sighed heavily. "Well, we have a little problem there. Let me tell you my story now ... "

Jon was keen to confront the strangers and evict them straight away. Understandably, Dan was more reticent about the prospect. As the three walked back towards their field, Gary tried to reason with his headstrong friend.

"Look, Jon, these guys are nasty pieces of work. They tied you up and look what they did to Dan!"

"I'm not scared by a couple of nineteen seventies hippies, they can't do this to us!"

As they approached the tent, Gary had a deep sense of foreboding. However, just before they got there, a couple of heavily tattooed men, with gnarled faces, heavy beards and hollow eyes intercepted them. Both of them looked frightening, almost like zombies.

The first man seized Dan by the collar. "Hey you, creeps, what are you doing here? Have you stolen our tent?" His voice had the texture of broken glass.

"No, no, of course not," Jon intervened, "We're just passing through, guys, we're not looking for trouble."

The second man spoke, in a low, chesty growl. "This is our spot, we have been coming to this festival every year since the mid-sixties ... "

"You will find two men inside your tent," Gary enjoyed making his contribution to the discussion. "Why don't you have a word with them - perhaps it's time they left ... "

As the friends strolled away from the field for the final time, Gary felt strangely elated.

"Don't worry, lads, I'm sure we'll find somewhere to sleep tonight before we head home tomorrow. I fancy a few beers and some fun myself now, and I think I might know where there's a card game ..."

Relationships

Anon

For couples so eager to call it quits after the infatuation wears off, to throw in the towel on there relationship because everything isn't 'perfect'... here is some food for thought. Lifelong commitment is not what most people think it is. It's not waking up every morning to make breakfast and eat together. It's not cuddling in bed until both of you fall asleep. It's not a clean home, filled with laughter and love making every day. It's someone who steals all the covers, and snores, it's slammed doors and a few harsh words at times. It's stubbornly disagreeing and giving each other the silent treatment until your hearts heal, and then offering forgiveness. It's coming home to the same person every day that you know loves and cares about you in spite of, and because of, who you are. It's laughing about the one time you accidentally did something stupid. It's about dirty laundry and unmade beds. It's about helping each other with the hard work of life. It's about swallowing the nagging words instead of saying them out loud. It's about eating the easiest meal you can make and sitting down together at a late hour because you both had a crazy day. It's when you have an emotional breakdown and your love lays down with you and holds you, and tells you everything is going to be okay. And you believe them. It's about still loving someone even though sometimes they make you absolutely insane. Loving someone isn't always easy, sometimes it's hard. But it is amazing and comforting and one of the best things you will ever experience

The Last Day (1)

Trudie Oakley

Dan leant against the wall in his stinking squat oblivious to the pungent smell of urine and mice droppings. He was just coming down from his last fix and his world had never been so utterly dark and miserable.   He winced as he ran his bruised fingers under his dripping nose. The fingers and the cuts around his eye were reminders that Markov meant business and today was his last chance to settle up. The Romanian loan shark had a formidable reputation and he trembled violently as he thought about the consequences of failing to pay. This was probably his last day on this earth! He slid to the floor and lay in a foetal position – maybe it would be a blessed relief from the living hell that had been his existence for the last few months.

As he lay awaiting his fate his mind drifted back to the good days; the days when he had been a promising student and had gained a place at the prestigious local Grammar School. His parents had been so proud of him and they like him, had been full of ambition for his future. His favourite master used to tell him that for a boy with his talents the world was his oyster and he could do anything that he set his mind to. He was happy then, he was set on a privileged course to success; that is until he met Josh Rawlings.

Josh moved into the area when Dan was in his third year and he seemed to Dan to be everything that he had wanted to aspire to. He had a confidence that so often accompanies children from well to do families.   He was great fun and seemed so sophisticated and for some reason which mystified Dan, Josh sought him out as a friend.   Dan was soon under the older boy's thrall and as a consequence he began to argue with his parents who were worried at the change in their son. From being an 'A' student they began receiving reports that Daniel was not doing his homework and was frequently truanting.

As Dan lay in the surrounding squalor he had to admit to himself that meeting Josh had been his downfall. He had been encouraged to smoke cannabis which had inevitably lead on to harder and more expensive drugs. He had been expelled from school and, purely to fund his by now well entrenched addiction, had taken a string of dead end jobs until even that was more than he could be bothered with, and that was when he hit rock bottom. It didn't matter to him where the money came from. Shoplifting, house breaking, stealing from his family – he didn't care just as long as he could get his drugs.

Despite entreaties from his parents he would not admit to how low he had fallen and so, in order to protect their other children, they had cast him off. He had drifted from squat to squat concerned only with feeding his insatiable need for drugs, and in their small town every road to narcotics involved Markov. Dan had done his bidding for a while but got further and further into debt until Markov's patience had run out, and after giving him a taste of what it meant to incur his displeasure had given just two days to pay up.

Dan felt along his brow with his damaged fingers and thought about yesterday when he had gone back home. His father had answered the door and had been unable to hide the shock and disgust at the sight of his once beloved son who had changed beyond all recognition. He stepped out and closed the door behind him. "Dear Lord Daniel, what on earth have you come to? Just look at you!"

Dan wrapped his arms around his knees more tightly and began to sob as he thought of their encounter. "I don't want a lecture Dad, I just need money. There's this man and if I don't pay him £500 by tomorrow I'm ..."

His father had been furious "How dare you come round here demanding money! You're throwing your life down the toilet and you expect me to help! I've got three other children who are worth caring for, but you! You are on a one way ticket to self destruction." His voice rose "And you seriously expect me to help you? No son, you've made your bed and now you'll have to take the consequences – now go; I'd hate your mother to see you like this."

Dan turned to go shouting "That's right! At least I've got a life not just the humdrum waste of years that yours has turned out to be. Just stick your money and I hope you choke on it."

So here he was awaiting his fate on what was probably his last day on earth. He drifted off still with arms wrapped around curled knees but was woken by a heavy kick to his shins. Markov and his sidekick Sonny stood over him. He was kicked again, it hurt like hell but he could do nothing, he had given up and just lay quietly ready to accept his fate.

Suddenly Markov was on the mattress beside him – he couldn't make sense of it. A vice like grip clamped onto his arm, "Come on son. Stand up and be a man!"

His senses cleared and he saw his dad, but this didn't make sense. He looked down at a prone Markov whose nose was gushing blood. He saw notes flutter down, some sticking on the congealing mess. "There's your money you bastard, and if I ever hear that you've threatened my son again, I'll kill you, and that is a promise."

Sonny stood by not moving. This was not supposed to happen and he wasn't sure what to do. He was paid for his brawn but this situation required brains and that was out of his league, so he watched in silence doing nothing.

Dan's father grabbed both of his arms, pushed him hard against a graffiti covered wall and slapped him around both sides of his face before grabbing hold of it and staring hard into his eyes.

"No ifs or buts now son, you are going into a clinic and you aren't bloody well coming out until you are clean and can see some sense."

Daniel was confused "But how did you know...."

"Do you think I haven't kept my eye on you all this time? Did you honestly think I would abandon you to that low life? I just had to wait until you came to me – until you couldn't get any lower."

Dan's emotions were running riot. "But you whacked him Dad. You put him down! How did you. I mean I didn't know you could do that."

He felt a strong arm supporting him as he left behind the squat and his old miserable life "There's a lot you don't know about me son; you've just never bothered to ask."

**

Ireland

Janette Menday

With the sun rising just above the hills, they sat side by side on the rocky outcrop, breathing in the sea air and tasting the salt on their lips. They were gazing down onto the vast collection of stones which together looked like a giant honeycomb dramatically strewn into the water.

"Ach, you must know the story behind these stones don't you?" he asked her, his strong vocal inflection betraying his northern Irish roots, so different from her soft welsh lilt.

"I believe I do, but tell me yours," she answered.

"Well, Finn MacCool was a gentle giant living with his wife in these parts long long ago. At 52 feet and six inches he was a relatively small giant. Now Finn was having trouble with Benandonner, the Scottish giant across the water, who was threatening peaceful Ireland. Finn was ragin' so he grabbed chunks of the Antrim coast and threw them into the sea. The rocks formed a path for Finn to follow all the way to Scotland to teach Benandonner a lesson.

"Aye sure why nat? – but Benandonner was terrifyingly massive and when Finn saw the size of him he fled back home. Benandonner followed Finn across the causeway to his home in Ireland. There he saw Finn, disguised as a wee baby by his quick-thinking wife".

"You'll be wanting Finn," said the wife, "He'll be coming along shortly."

"The angry Scot stared at the baby and decided if the child was that huge, the daddy must be extraordinarily colossal. Benandonner was so scared, so he was, that he beat a hasty retreat back to Scotland, destroying most of the path to ensure Finn could never follow him. And that's how and why the Giants Causeway was created."

"Extraordinary" she replied, "but I have a story about these rocks that is even more magical and awesome!" She smiled shyly.

He laughed, "I can't wait, tell me!"

She paused and stared out at the rocks. Then she spoke softly. "Like many places on the planet millions of years ago, there was intense volcanic activity here. Highly fluid molten rock was forced up through fissures in the chalk beds of the earth, disgorging into the sea. The water churned and steamed and hissed like a herd of angry dragons.

"Segments of lava flow began to cool, contracting, and fracturing, creating the hexagonal shaped basalt columns you see there." She turned to face him, "These stones are the aftermath of volcanic crashing, burning and cooling, an epic 60-million-year-old legacy and turning to lava. Over 40,000 basalt columns, all interlocked. And that is nature at its most breathtaking."

"That's a grand story", he said amazed, "even more unbelievable than Finn MacCool".

"That", she replied, "is the awesome wonder of physics and science".

**

An English professor wrote the words:

"A woman without her man is nothing" on the chalkboard and asked the students to punctuate it correctly.

All of the males in the class wrote:
"A woman, without her man, is nothing."

All of the females in the class wrote:
"A woman: without her, man is nothing."

Punctuation is powerful.

The Lady with the Lamp

By Richard Seal

"I attribute my success to this - I never gave or took any excuse." - Florence Nightingale

Florence Nightingale was a pioneering figure in nursing who had a huge impact on 19th and 20th century policies around patient care and health reform. She was born in May 1820, in Florence, Italy. Nightingale was the younger of two children, and hers was an affluent British family. From a very young age, the girl was keen to look after the sick and poor people in the village close to her family's estate. By the time she was in her mid-teens she believed that nursing was her God-given calling. Her parents were unimpressed, but in 1844 the determined young woman enrolled as a nursing student at the Lutheran Hospital of Pastor Fliedner in Kaiserwerth, Germany.

In the early 1850s, Nightingale returned to England and took a nursing job in a London hospital, where her impressive work saw her promoted to superintendant within a year. It was a very challenging position as she attempted to improve hygiene practices during a cholera outbreak. In 1853, the Crimean War broke out, and within twelve months thousands of soldiers were languishing in understaffed, appallingly unsanitary military hospitals. At the time, there were no female nurses stationed in the Crimea. However, in late 1854, Secretary of War Sidney Herbert called for Florence's help. She quickly assembled a team of 34 nurses, and they sailed within a few days.

Conditions at Scutari, the British base hospital in Constantinople, were horrendous. A cesspool contaminated the water and the hospital building, while patients lay in their own excrement on stretchers in hallways. Bandages and soap grew increasingly scarce, and water needed to be rationed. More soldiers were dying from typhoid and cholera than from battle injuries. Florence set the least infirm patients to work scrubbing the inside of the hospital, while she spent all her time caring for the soldiers. In the evenings she moved through the hallways carrying a lamp while looking after her patients, and the men took to calling her "the Lady with the Lamp" or "the Angel of the Crimea." Her work reduced the hospital's death rate by two-thirds.

In addition to the vast improvement to the sanitary conditions, Nightingale ensured that food for patients with special dietary requirements could be prepared, and she established a laundry, a classroom and a library. Florence's report 'Notes on Matters Affecting the Health, Efficiency and Hospital Administration of the British Army' analysed her Crimea experience and proposed reforms for other military hospitals. Further to the book's publication, the War Office's administrative department was restructured and a Royal Commission for the Health of the Army was established in 1857. Nightingale remained at Scutari for eighteen months. Returning home in 1856, she was surprised to be met with a hero's welcome. The Queen presented her with an engraved brooch.

Nightingale's health would never fully recover from her experiences at Scutari. By the end of her thirties she was largely bedridden, but she remained as dedicated to her work as ever. Now living in London, she continued to be an advocate of and authority in health reform. In 1859, she published 'Notes on Hospitals', and the following year she established St. Thomas' Hospital, and the Nightingale Training School for Nurses. Throughout the U.S. Civil War, Florence was consulted about how best to manage field hospitals, and she advised on public sanitation issues in India. Florence became a figure who was widely admired by the public, and thanks to her, nursing came to be regarded as an honourable and heroic vocation.

In 1908, Florence was conferred the merit of honour by King Edward, and two years later received a congratulatory message from King George on her 90th birthday. A few months later, on 13 August, she died peacefully at home in Mayfair. Respecting her last wishes, a national funeral was turned down, and the "Lady with the Lamp" was laid to rest in a family plot. The Florence Nightingale Museum, located at the site of the original Nightingale Training School, contains more than 2,000 artifacts which commemorate the life and career of the "Angel of the Crimea." She is still acknowledged and revered as the trailblazer of modern nursing.

**

"Have a heart that never hardens, and a temper that never tires, and a touch that never hurts." — Charles Dickens

Growing food Efficiently

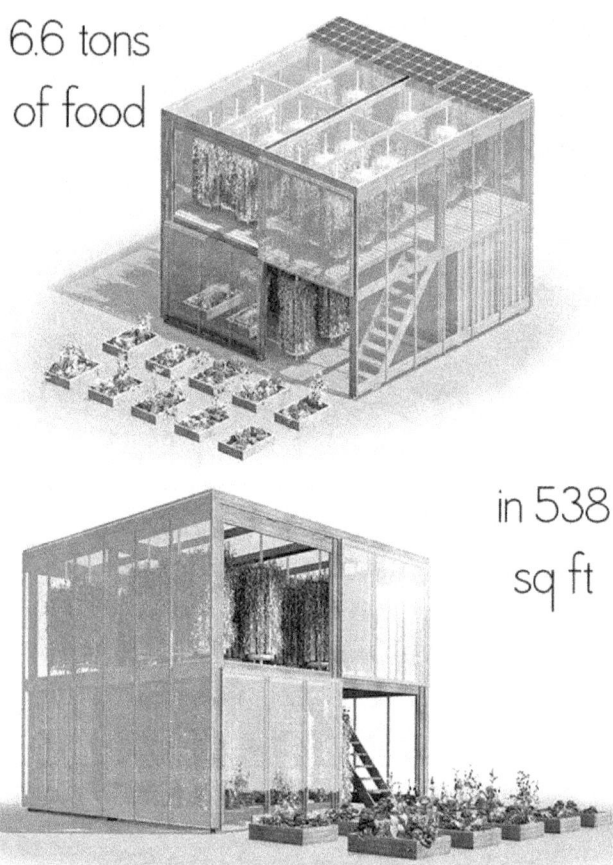

6.6 tons of food

in 538 sq ft

Mums Handbag

Caroline Goss

Everyone joked when I bought Mum a handbag,
It was bigger and bluer that the old one she had.
All sorts of things could be hid there that Mum liked
to save,
It was like delving into a big black cave!

But Mum always found just what she could,
Why not ask her, I think you should?
The big, blue, bag of compartments and zips,
Straps and buckles, poppers and clips!

You'd never believe what she had in that bag,
From plasters to screwdrivers and shop cards to
brag!
Keys and pins and crystal charms,
Along with a tape measure as long as your arms!

The remnants of forgotten pills,
And bags of sweets to have your fill,
Perfume, sticky tape and a pair of tights,
Even a torch to light up the night,

Pencils, crayons and Tipex too,
Also paper to use in the loo!
A worn out comb, a few hair grips,
A half eaten packet of salt and vinegar crisps!

Cuttings from the newspaper, her favourite verse,
Not forgetting her blue leather purse,
Credit cards, debit cards and the Tesco's card for
points,
Even some cream for her achy joints!

Shopping lists written on old bits of card,
Trying to find them was terribly hard.
Polo mints and a mobile phone,
Buttons and thread which Mum kept on their own.

Occasionally she'd sort her bag out if she had time,
But to us her bag was just fine,
Scattering the table with all its contents,
But for us it is what it represents ....

The heart of the bag and everything in it,
Was in Mums soul and the light that it lit.
She had all of these things,
In her body and mind,
And gave us her love to which we did find,
Her own treasure chest was abundant with love,
And for each one of us Mum shares from above.

Mums handbag a rare delight,
Just like an Aladdin's Cave'
All sorts of things are hidden there,
With all the love a mother can share.

The Pearl

Janne Tarika Gravdal

Many years ago before mother was born, Grandma bought an island outside Bergen in Norway. Mother grew up there, and we celebrated the summer holidays there every year.

There we were, on the small fine beaches, swimming, fishing, looked at the starry sky in the evening, and I had my own secret place in the middle of the island, at least I thought it was secret.

My grandmother died when I was three and the grandmother's house was vandalized. All furnishings, ceilings, walls and windows were broken. So, every holiday after that we were in a tent until I was 8, when my father built a new house, further down to the sea. We didn't have any water or electricity. So without any other light around, the starry sky was amazing.

But the years we lay in the tent, was so exciting, The sound of when it rained on the roof of the tent and sometimes in the nights we could hear and see earth mice running over the tent. There were lots of sounds of different animals in the night, and the music of the sea, that was splashing against land.

Right from the time I was a little kid, I trickled out at 6 o'clock in the morning, took the boat and rowed out and fished. It was absolutely enchanting, the steam rising up from the sea and the fish biting. After a couple of hours, I rowed to shore and made a fire by the seaside, took a pan and filled it with seawater. As I waited for the water to boil, I opened the fish and made it clean. When the fish was cooked, I took a potato from the day before, spread butter over it and ate it all with my hands. Something fresher and more delicious you cannot get. It was a great time.

Every year when the summer vacation was over I was already looking forward to the next summer on the Island, so I could swim, fish, and hide at my secret place, and in the evenings look at all the stars, and be filled with energy.

The Island was, and is, and will forever be my pearl.

**

"I'm very proud of my gold pocket watch. My grandfather, on his deathbed, sold me this watch" - Woody Allen

The Last Day (2)

Percy Chattey

Seating in the corner with his back to the engine, he had been told it was safer to travel that way, was a young man watching the green countryside flashing past the carriage, it was was rocking slightly with the momentum as with a deep hum and the noise of the trains multi numbered wheels, it raced across the railway tracks. Suddenly there would be an increase in the sound, thunderous and reverberating as the InterCity monster hurried, nonstop through a station, before the previous echoes settled down again to their original rhythm. On these occasions he would pull back in surprise from the unexpected darkened window.

Sitting on the upright dull beige coloured brocade seat, Adam was leaning against the side and continues staring out of the grubby window, mesmerised by the scenery, dotted with trees and hedgerows and the infrequent farmhouse. Occasionally a small group of houses would be nestling in amongst the landscape, whilst in some of the fields, dressed in floppy hats, shading them from the sun and dressed in different types of denim's people were gathering the harvest, they looked up briefly as his means of transport propelled him onwards.

Whilst watching the vista as it flashed past his mind was thinking of the bygone days ... was it really three years since he was on a similar but different train going in the opposite direction? He remembered it well. School years were behind him and the future was looking bleak as he strayed from one type of uninteresting employment to another. It was an unpleasant day and he was on his way home feeling a little down, when he saw the Army Recruitment Centre, and out of impulse, he went in.

It had been the right decision at the time, one with no regrets, except one? Adam could feel strong emotions and a misting of his sight, he brushed the moisture away with the back of his hand which had formed on his cheek, as he recalled laughing hazel eyes, although she insisted, they were green, set in a lovely face smiling at him.

He remembered before that momentous occasion the thrill of discarding his old ways, the interesting times full of exciting events and travel as the Regiment he had been assigned to, taught him new skills and changed his life. It was a man's world full of adventure meeting new friends and travelling the planet.

The carriage door slid open and a person entered from the corridor. He turned, his heart missed a beat, she was blond she smiled at him taking a seat at the far end. He relaxed and returned to the window as he realised the newcomer looked nothing like the person he was reminiscing over.

The rhythm of the train disappeared as his thoughts went back, he had been delegated to the Head Quarters of the signals unit he belonged to. An office job! But how could he forget his first day - he was in a line with others of the new intake who had just arrived waiting to be assigned accommodation. He had been chatting to the fellow behind him when he got to the front and turned. She was sitting behind a desk and lifted her head and smiled, her blond hair beautifully formed around her head. His mouth had gone dry and he found his hand shaking as he passed his papers over to her. In dismay he noticed the 'Pips' on her shoulder's he knew instantly they would be in the way of getting to know her better, Officers did not mix with the lower ranks.

He was lucky in the posting, about a thousand miles away, in that it was in the warmth. It was a small Army Unit attached to a working division. As time went by, he would frequently see her during the day and she would go out of her way to acknowledge him. They became very close in this odd situation and as they sometimes worked together in the Signals Office, both could feel the natural comfortable pull to the other.

It was Christmas time and there was a relaxed atmosphere at the social gathering organised by the Senior ranks. The Regiment's Band was playing and the Commissioned Officers were prepared to mix on this one occasion. Adam was stunned when she asked him to dance and for the first time his dream had come to reality as she glided around the floor in his arms. It was on this occasion she told him the Unit was going back home soon but she would let him know how to get in touch with her.

The time came for the Entity to relocate back to the United Kingdom. It was the last day and the senior ranks were due to leave first. He was in his office with two others carrying out some final packing. They heard a jeep squeal and stop outside. She came in and put a file on his desk. She looked at the others who had their backs to her. The lieutenant winked saying, "you need to deal with that immediately". She allowed a smile to creep over her face and quickly turned and left.

The train rumbled on. Adam was now smiling to himself as he felt into his top pocket and retrieved the frayed note caused by his constant studying of it. It was in her neat handwriting which he recognised immediately, she had left it for him on that last day. A simple few words with an address in Southern England, he was sure it was the town they had just rushed past. Would he go back?

There was a sound behind him and he realised the other person was speaking and had said "Excuse me!" Adam turned. She was comfortably seated in the far corner, relaxed and half turned in his direction. His eyes naturally wandered over her before settling on her face. Her blue eyes searched out his and they locked together. "I'm on my way to London, I am wondering how long it will take because I have never been before." A pair of dimples touched her cheeks, before adding "Do you know it well?"

There was something in her voice which made him think there was more. He felt the note in his hand and gently squeezed it into a small ball and put it in the ash tray.

Summary Holidays

...and this was just the first day!

Caroline Goss

"I want to leave in fifteen minutes at the latest." Bev didn't really take any notice of Mike as he shouted out to her whilst strapping his fishing gear onto the roof bars of the car.

Bev finished tidying up the kitchen after an early morning breakfast and quite aware of the time. "It's my holiday as well and I'm the one that's always left tidying up the house," she muttered under her breath! Bev didn't have much room in the car it was packed to the hilt! Her feet were enveloped in bags of last minute food from the fridge. Even poor old Jasper secured to his leash on the back seat was surrounded by feather duvets and pillows. Mike was the only one who had the ring side seat because he was driving!

Ten minutes into the journey Mike suddenly shouted, "Oh no", and with an angry grimace on his face Bev knew he had forgotten something. "I forgot my box of weights and all the hooks, I'm going to have to go back and get them!"

Bev raised her eyebrows from the passenger seat, which she knew that Mike wouldn't see, and she was just about to say something but thought better of it as she wanted a peaceful holiday without any drama!

Once back at the house Jasper started to bark and leap about as much as he could under the restraint of the lead and the restrictions of all the bedding. He was getting very excited because he knew exactly where he was and was probably thinking that was a short journey. The excitement of the dog didn't help the situation as Mike was frantically trying to unlock the gate leading to the driveway.

Eventually the threesome carried on their journey and it was decided if anything else was forgotten then they would not go back for it. Bev knew she was pretty much in the clear here as she had everything she wanted planned and executed methodically as it was packed!

The M25 was nose to tail as they travelled at a snail's pace through the Hertfordshire country side. It was so stuffy and the amount of vehicles on the hot asphalt road didn't help. All the windows were down to their fullest and Jasper enjoyed what breeze he could. Stop start, stop start it was a nightmare. Then they heard a buzzing sound in the car. Was it a wasp? Was it a bee? No! It was a hornet!

Jasper was very excited about their new passenger and was snapping away merrily trying to catch it. Bev picked up a magazine bought to read on the journey trying to usher it out the window as Mike was trying his best to drive the car dodging his head and thrashing his arm about. Other drivers passing in their cars were looking at this somewhat demented family as if they were dancing to the latest House music. One car driver even took great delight in tooting his horn as their passengers shouted out the window, joining in!

Finally, the raging beast flew like a torpedo out the window but not before Mike yelled a mighty scream! 'It's stung me on my arm'. The car veered slightly to the left of the middle lane and other cars started to hoot.

He managed to regain control of the car as Bev rummaged around in her bag to find something to help with the sting. Mike was grimacing and sweat was beating his brow now as he tried to concentrate on driving. There was nothing Bev could find to ease the sting but a small block of stilton cheese which was in the freezer bag around her feet. Mike didn't care what it was he just needed something cool!

"Look there's the sign for the services we'll stop there!" She knew Mike hated stopping at these places but this was an emergency and Mike needed some respite.

It seemed an age to get there as Mike was battling the pain of the sting! Once at the Service Station they followed car after car going around in circles. 'That cars driving out I'll go and stand in the spot," Bev jumped out of the car and as if in some sort of obstacle race she darted around the cars to stand boldly in the now vacant parking slot.

Mike drove in but not without a gruff looking driver shouting abuse at him as he wanted that space! Mike didn't care and although the pain was beginning to ease off a huge blister began to form on his arm. Luckily once in the service station there was a First Aid point and an elderly man proudly displaying his First Aiders badge immediately attended Mike's sting. The cream applied was such a relief to Mike, the pain subsided and the blister began to fade.

Finally, they got back to the car and a mass of feathers blew out from the draft of opening the door! Jasper had been having a grand time in their absence; the car was strewn with feathers from the duvet! Like little feathered angels the feathers spiralled up into the open air and drifted aimlessly across the bevy of parked cars in the heat of the midday sun! The duvet was completely torn open but Jasper didn't care as he wagged his tail and tongue hanging out glad to see his masters.

"Don't shout at him! It's our fault and if you hadn't got stung we wouldn't have stopped and this wouldn't have happened", Bev was quick to defend Jasper. "Let's just get on with the rest of our journey and sort this out when we get there".

Mike had calmed down from the episode at the service station and as they were nearing their destination they both began to feel excited. The flat terrain of the tree lined lane was a far cry from the busy motorway as it twisted its way to the boat yard where they would soon be starting their holiday.

Suddenly Bev felt something irritating her neck as she sat there in the car. She brushed it aside. A few minutes later she felt the same thing and again brushed it aside with her hand and as she turned round to see if it was Jasper she noticed something crawling on the dishevelled duvet. She half hitched herself up from her seat and didn't see just one but hundreds of shrivelled up crawling fluorescent maggots with nowhere to go! "Mike!" she yelled. Mike immediately slammed on the brakes and the car came to a sudden halt throwing the duvet forward and all the maggots were thrown forward through the car.

Panic ensued as both Mike and Bev leapt out of the car throwing open the doors as they scrambled out tearing off their clothes and shaking their hair to get rid of the grubby little maggots. A lady on a bicycle rode down the dusty lane giving the dancing couple a quizzical look and decided not to stop and get involved, *it could be drugs*, she alarmingly thought to herself and sped off as fast as her little legs could cycle!

The maggots dropped out of their clothes and hair, crawling away up the verge of the road as if in a race. Then it was Jaspers turn. Jasper thought it was great fun being brushed from head to foot with both their hands, *tummy rub time!*

"Whatever were you thinking putting the box of maggots for your fishing on the back seat with all the bedding?" Bev was livid as she was struggling with a tangle of sawdusty hair. "Jasper obviously smelt the grubs whilst we were in the service station hence the wrecked duvet as he was trying to seek them out. He must have dislodged the lid and they've all crawled out they're everywhere."

Mike had actually never seen his Bev so cross. But his eyes caught hers and as he looked at her almost half naked body with dishevelled hair sweeping across her face, he couldn't help having that glint in his eye. And he noticed the corners of her lips curl upwards with the little dimples on her cheeks as she started to laugh. She picked a grub wriggling its way back into his hair and he started laughing too.

They sorted themselves out shook out the duvet and continued the remainder of their journey. At last they had arrived. Jasper could sense the excitement and as soon as he was unleashed started to race around all over the place.

"Oh no Jasper!" It was too late Jasper had jumped into a very green weedy looking part of the river. "He thought it was grass, quick we'd better rescue him!" Jasper was very shocked about getting so wet but loved the water and soon swam and scrambled up the muddy side. "Look at the state of us all" Bev didn't know whether to laugh or cry.

That evening Bev and Mike chugged along the quiet river on their little boat and found an idyllic spot under a weeping willow tree to tie up. They were sat on the deck watching the sun go down behind the line of poplar trees swaying gently in the warm summer breeze. The chirp of the crickets in the meadow and the croak of a distant frog broke the silence as they watched the butterflies finding shelter for the night amongst the tall grasses. And with a glass of wine and Jasper by their side toasted the start of their summer holiday.

"To our summer holiday," they both touched glasses with a melodic chink just as the boat slipped its mooring to which they were quite oblivious .... but that's another story!

To all the Mummy's

Who don't look the way they used to.
Not feeling as confident as they used to.

Whose photos are of their beautiful babies instead of selfies because you can't find a filter to fix the tired eyes or get a decent angle anymore.

To all the Mums that feel like they have lost their identity. All those who feel like they have lost friends along the way.

To the ones who forget what day of the week it is and can't remember the last time you had a bath or toilet break alone.

I just want to tell you that you are amazing! So strong and beautiful.

And that it's okay to cry and crave just 20 minutes alone. You are a superstar... even if you don't always feel like it.

Being a Mum is hard work and constant.

Every day you make it work and get up the next day to do it all again. Be proud of yourself.

Every day you become stronger and more inspiring to other Mums just trying to keep it together too.

Go Be Your Own Warrior

Anon

**

My grandpa started walking five miles a day when he was 60. Now he's 97 years old and we don't know where the heck he is.

Box

Richard Seal

For a large part of his working life Michael spent his time feeling trapped, cramped up in a tiny tight box, which seemed to shrink more and more with each passing year; the man's limbs became increasingly contorted, his back twisted, bent over in pain, barely able to breathe, there was no sign of relief ...

In his early years as a contract manager, Michael would enjoy travelling out to meet enthusiastic project leaders who were so keen to share their passion for their respective Government-funded programmes. Jaunty types with rolled-up sleeves proudly shared tales of men long unemployed who had had their aspirations raised by newly-created training or job opportunities, while isolated individuals became connected and engaged through a range of innovative community activities. The Civil Servant's visits involved unbridled positivity, declarations of joy and cups of tea and handshakes with grateful beneficiaries. The occasional target milestone missed was not worried about overmuch given that so much else had been done, and great things achieved could not always be easily counted.

Over time he witnessed things slowly beginning to change for the worse, as various funding streams dried up or got much tighter, while targets and output measures became rigidly-enforced, prescribed and strictly evidence-based. Michael knew that he had no appetite to make the transition from 'the friendly face of the Agency' with a reputation for having a flexible, pragmatic approach and conducting 'high-level project walk -throughs', to a hatchet- faced 'bean counter' on a monitoring visit, armed with audit checklists, and a potent threat to withhold or even claw back the funding. The man's energy and will drained away with each successive restriction and limitation to the scope of his role.

However, one day his spirits raised a little at being asked to re-visit the local museum and art gallery in Pontown. Michael had helped the original capital project to secure additional funding for a new wing to house a Pop-Art collection, with the grant dependent on creating a number of new jobs and learning opportunities. Michael made a point of arriving early to give himself time to walk around and see the displays alone. He fondly recalled the project manager's happiness at the prospect of being able to extend the facilities for the benefit of the local community. When Frank had shaken his hand on receiving the news of the financial approval there had been tears in his eyes.

To his slight disappointment, Michael was not met by Frank, but instead encountered an equally personable and effervescent young man called Ian, who pumped his outstretched hand vigorously.

"Hello, Michael, it's wonderful to meet you."

"Thanks, Ian, you too." He put down his heavy briefcase and straightened his back. "It's been a long time .. "

"Yes it has. I'm sorry that Frank's gone now, he retired last year, but I phoned to tell him that you were coming to visit us and he sends you his very best regards."

"That's nice, please give him mine too. I remember Frank very well of course.

"He enjoys his gardening and golf, but I know he misses the gallery very much and would come back and join us if he could, I'm sure."

Ian enthusiastically gave his visitor a full walking tour and relished showing off the impressive Pop Art displays.

"It's great isn't it? And none of this would have been possible without the financial support of your Department! Thank you so much."

Michael smiled. "Has the gallery extension and new exhibition been popular with the local community, have visitor numbers increased as expected?"

A hint of doubt had crept into the young man's expression. "Well there were a lot more people when it first opened, I think, but the numbers seem to have evened off over time .. Shall we sit down and have a chat over coffee?"

Sitting in the small office, the last thing Michael really wanted to do was take out his audit checklist and a copy of the guidance note for evidencing output measures.

"I sent a copy of these to you, or rather to Frank, some time ago."

Ian tried, without success, to conceal his uncertainty. "Okay .. Is everything satisfactory?"

Michael looked at him sombrely. "I hope so, Ian, I really do. Tell me, has all the project funding been spent now?"

"Oh yes, no problems there at all, everything was claimed to profile, I am pleased to report!"

"That's great. Now has there been any problem achieving the job creation and learning opportunity output targets? I haven't seen a project monitoring return for some time. Has there been some slippage?"

Ian looked blank, before recovering some of his composure. "Well, my job has been created and the visitors have learned a lot from the new displays .. "

"The application stated that learning workshops would be held, and training days delivered in the new classroom space connected to the gallery extension. Frank told me that he had various ideas about how to achieve these targets. Has this happened?"
Ian looked at him forlornly. "I don't really know too much about that, I don't think so. Would you like to see the project files?"

Michael had no genuine desire to inspect the paperwork, but dearly hoped that the files would shed a more positive light on the situation. To his dismay, there was little evidence of note and certainly nothing remotely in line with the guidance. Virtually none of the contracted outputs had been achieved.

"I'm sorry if the records aren't perfect, Michael, but you must agree that the new gallery is a wonderful facility and the artworks are impressive ... All the people tell us that they love them."

The contract manager closed the file, sat in silence for a moment and closed his eyes. He knew it wouldn't be long before a headache took hold.

"There's no problem is there?" The man looked at him imploringly. "Do you have any more questions?"

Michael could barely bring himself to consider the next course of punitive action. This visit and the man's desperate expression proved to be the straw which broke the camel's back.

****

Michael whistles cheerfully to himself, as he so often likes to do, whilst pushing the wheelchair towards the operating theatre. He smiles at the elderly patient who is currently in his care:

"How are you doing down there, Phyllis? Are you enjoying the ride? Am I going quickly enough for you?"

"It's better than travelling on the bus, my dear, thank you for looking after me."

"The pleasure is all mine."

"Do you enjoy your job Michael? You certainly sound happy."

"Talking to lovely ladies like yourself, Phyllis, what's not to enjoy? It's a physical job, I spend some of my time moving equipment, patient files and other things around the hospital, which keeps me fit, but I enjoy working with people the most."

"Well, you're helping me to keep my spirits up."

"I'm very glad to hear it. We're nearly there now, how are you feeling?"

"A bit nervous, but I know it will be better for me after the operation."

"Of course it will, you will feel as right as rain in no time. I will bring you a special lunch tomorrow to celebrate . Do you have any requests?"

"Oh I'm happy with anything really, to be honest. Meat and two veg?"

"Okay, I'll see what I can do. It will be a special surprise banquet, just for you."

"Thanks again, Michael, you're a piece of gold." She holds his hand for a moment before they part company.

The man stands for a few moments, reflecting on the extended break he had taken after spending more than two decades in the Civil Service. He had been laid low with debilitating stress and nervous exhaustion, which only began to dissipate when he finally resigned and commenced his new life as a Hospital Porter eighteen months previously. Michael now loves coming to work every day, and gets a genuine buzz from his contact with patients and colleagues. He relishes the rising sensation of elation and the thrilling surge of adrenalin rush as he heads back to the ward for his next assignment.

The next day Phyllis is beaming when she sees the Porter approaching with her dinner tray.

"Hello Phyllis, and how are you feeling today? You're looking as fit as a fiddle. Have they let you start playing rugby yet?"

"No, I think that might need to wait for a little while. I'm feeling really good, though, just as you predicted. Not too sore at all."

"Wonderful. Well, as promised, I was planning to bring you a three course meal today, with prawn cocktail, caviar, champagne and all the trimmings ... But I'm afraid that I ended up eating it all myself .. So we have some tasty cottage pie for you instead."

"My favourite, Michael, where would I be without you?" She pointed her spoon at him. "If you carry on being a good boy, I might save you some of my apple crumble and custard"

"I'm looking forward to it already! Enjoy, dear Phyllis, and I'll see you later on."

... These days Michael's box looks so very different. It is much bigger, feels warm and cosy and has windows which he can open at any time to let in fresh air. This is a safe space, a comforting place where the man can enjoy his private time in peace, letting off steam, re-energising. No longer desiring to flee, this captive has been set free.

**

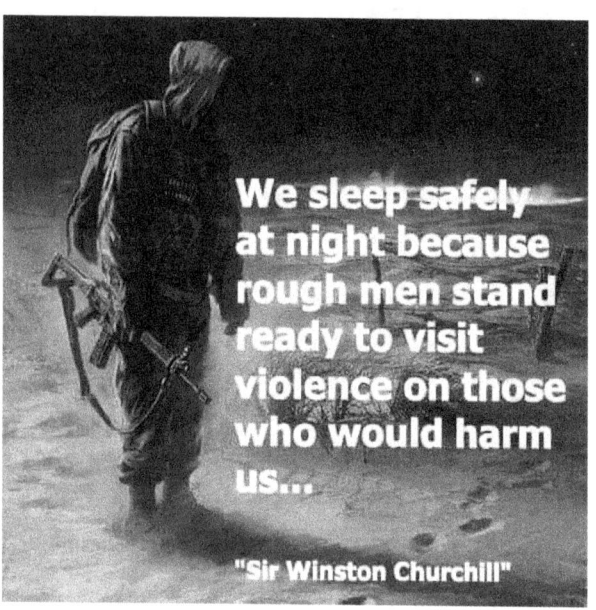

**

A SIGN IN A
SHOE REPAIR STORE IN VANCOUVER READS:
We will heel you. We will save your sole.
We will even dye for you.

Benidorm, Costa Blanca, Spain

Lee Halliday

I must admit visiting Benidorm has never been on my agenda. In fact, as a family we have done everything to avoid such busy places. On our regular visits to Moraira, we used to gasp at the tower blocks as we drove from the airport towards the Northern Costa Blanca, in disbelief that people would want a holiday surrounded by enormous sky scrapers. As a Travel Agent many years ago, pensioners would be queuing at the door as the winter brochures went on sale for the 18 week holidays for a miserly few hundred pounds half board. Often these types of holidays were booked up within 24 hours.

Over the years the TV programme 'Benidorm' became a huge hit and although I enjoyed the programme, it didn't do anything to influence my view that Benidorm was a place for stag do's and pensioners seeking a cheap life on a budget, with nonstop entertainment. I'm no longer 18 and I'm not yet ready for my pension so it doesn't tick any of my boxes.

Having moved to Spain and with my daughters love for the TV programme, (it's become seriously poor over the last few years but she still loves it), we promised her a visit.

Mother's Day arrived and somewhere in the UK we have always tried to spend time as a family, it was either Anglesey, Hebden Bridge in Yorkshire, the Cotswolds or the Lakes but with 'Bener's' being 1 hour away we thought lets go for it, in for a penny in for a pound. My daughter was excited – I wasn't.

I remember the people in Thomas Cook telling me the old town was nice so we headed towards Poniente beach and parked up.

On first impression, I was somewhat surprised. The beach and the views were lovely. Yes, I could see a few sky scrapers, but they seemed less imposing than they did on the motorway driving towards Javea.

We walked along the beach for 20 minutes towards the old town. We arrived at the marina and the shops and both my wife and myself looked at one another accepting that we've clearly been a pair of portentous snobs over the years.

My daughter was in her element and I must admit I was too. Walking past the busy side streets full of tapas bars I just didn't expect Benidorm to be like this.

We headed towards Levante beach and the bars became livelier. Suddenly things changed quite dramatically. Blokes, red from the sun and often bigger breasts than the women on hen do's and the music pumping from the bars – this was Blackpool in the eighties – we did a quick U turn.

Levante is not for us. Perhaps twenty years ago, but not now. We headed back to the old town and had a lovely menu del dia – starter, 2 mains, a desert and a drink for 11 euros and it was well worth the money.

We headed up to the church and the old pedestrian area and even though Levante wasn't for us, overall Benidorm is. I was really surprised how lovely the place is. The beaches are stunning and there's an atmosphere where people have realised that life is too bloody short to be serious so just let go and enjoy yourself.

I would caution that we did go in March, and I think even the old town would be too much for us in the peak season, but no longer will I be sticking my nose up at anyone suggesting a trip to Benidorm. The idea that anyone who visits this place lives off egg and chips, Roast dinners Monday to Sunday, has a blue rinse and drives a promenade scooter is more than a bit harsh and from now on I am proud to advocate our famous Spanish tourist resort, Benidorm.

We will be back and dare I say it, it may be the place for us once we join the 24/7 cardigan brigade.

**

A little known fact!!

Did You Know This About Leather Dresses?

**Do you know that when a woman wears a leather dress ,
a man's heart beats quicker, his throat goes dry,
he gets weak in the knees, And he begins to think totally
irrationally. Ever stop to wonder why ?
Well, it's easy ....**

the lady smells like a new car

The Last Day (3)
– Automation

Caroline Goss

I was reading just the other day
Within a decade is what they say
That robots will over rule our lives
Is this how scaremongering thrives!

Scientists and technicians work hand in hand
As millions of jobs throughout the land
Are slowly lost through Automation
Make way for the new revolution!

Technology is advancing at such speed
Where on earth is this all going to lead?
Computers and robots whatever next
Some it leaves happy but others vexed.

Waiter, Cleaners and Admin Staff
Even those that have a craft
Chefs and Plumbers and Factory Workers
But what a wonderful life for the shirkers!

All these jobs will be taken over
By metallic humanoids or a dog called Rover
As the army of robots take on these roles
Don't just stand there and take the dole.

People need to gain new skills
Especially if they want to pay the bills
March alongside the robot army
Don't leave it too late or else you'll go barmy!

Ever since man invented the wheel
Then it was iron, coal and steel
Then engines driven by water and steam
Now precision engineering with laser beams

The last day has come so here's to our future
Press that button and start your computer
Automation is the way to go
So we'd better get used to it and go with the flow!

**

'I CAN HEAR JUST FINE!'

Three retirees, each with a hearing loss, were
playing golf one fine March day.
One remarked to the other, 'Windy, isn't it?'
'No,' the second man replied, 'it's Thursday'
And the third man chimed in, 'So am I. Let's
have a beer.'

"Life is too short, hug a little longer, love a little stronger, forgive a little sooner and smile a little sweeter."

– Caroline Naoroji

**

A SIGN ON A BLINDS AND CURTAIN TRUCK:

"Blind man driving."

A **cowboy** *walked into a bar and ordered a whisky.*

When the bartender delivered the drink,
the cowboy asked, "Where is everybody ?"
The bartender replied, "They've gone to the hanging."
"Hanging? Who are they hanging ?"
"Brown Paper Pete," the bartender replied.
"What kind of a name is that ?" the cowboy asked.
"Well," said the bartender,
he wears a brown paper hat, brown paper shirt, brown
paper trousers, and brown paper shoes."
"How bizarre," said the cowboy.
"What are they hanging him for ?"
"Rustling," said the bartender

Door Knockers Please Note

This household charges $20 per minute to listen to sales pitches and or religious messages.
This charge is payable in advance.

By knocking on this door you signal your agreement with the terms outlined above

Tunnel

Richard Seal

The tunnel was just the way that Mike imagined it would be. All his life, he had imagined the time when he would find himself in this dark place, on a one way trip to somewhere else, unknown. As he stumbled along, he used the walls to steady himself. The man was unable to see where he was going, but it seemed as if there were obstacles and pieces of debris at his feet, and it was difficult to navigate his way around them at times.

As he turned a bend, he came upon something solid in his way. "Hello?" He could barely hear his own voice, "Who's there?" He reached out a hand, but could feel nothing.

"It's Gill, Mike ... Hey, slow down, take it easy. There's no need to rush here."

The man recognised his younger sister's voice. "Gill? What on Earth are you doing here?" He had seen her a couple of weeks previously at the cafe where they occasionally met for coffee, and she had seemed okay, albeit quiet and introspective as usual.

"I have always been in the darkness ... I come out of it for short periods every now and then, but this is where I find myself a lot of the time. I don't mind, it's not a problem."

"What are you talking about? You like your job, have your own flat, and some nice friends ... You're happy enough with life, aren't you?"

"Sure, sometimes, of course .. whatever happiness actually means. Look, I'm not dead, if that's what you're worried about. It is not always sad here, there can be a certain amount of comfort and warmth in the blackness too. A kind of security, familiarity. "

"I don't really understand ... "

"We all have lots of places that we can call home, don't you think?" Ask yourself where you really live, Mike. I don't mean the semi-detached house with Leanne in Ealing. Life is not so straightforward."

"What do you mean?"

"What does anything actually mean, dear brother? There is no such thing as objective reality. Now, keep going on your way and see where you end up."

Her voice became quieter, its tone softening. "Keep an open mind, just go with it."

"Will I see you again?"

"Of course you will. Don't doubt it."

After a while the tunnel began to feel a little warmer, the space seemed to be widening, and he found that he could see a little more - vague shapes, outlines. Mike was on the point of stopping to rest on what looked like a flat rock, when he became aware of an indistinct figure sitting nearby in an armchair. Mike approached cautiously, but words failed him.

"Hello, son, how are you?" The voice was faltering.

"Joe? Is that really you?" His father-in-law had died of a heart attack three weeks ago after a protracted period of ill-health. He had been watching TV in his favourite chair when it happened.

"Where are we, Mike, what's happening?"

"Well, I'm not sure, I was hoping that you might be able to tell me."

"How should I know? I'm not even sure how long I've been here - Where is Milly, is she okay? And Leanne?"

Mike reassured Joe that his wife and daughter were both fine and wondered if the man was aware of what had happened to him. He had always seemed to be frightened about the prospect of death and had avoided discussing the subject at all costs.

"How are you feeling, Joe, are you in pain?"

"No, not at all. I feel good. I think I must have had a long sleep, am I awake now or am I dreaming?" His voice started to tail off, he seemed to be dozing off.

"It's a nice dream, enjoy it. Get some more rest, and I'll catch up with you later."

"Okay, son, give my love to everyone. God bless."

As Mike continued to walk he could feel some fresh air coming in from somewhere, and an occasional shaft of daylight appeared through the odd crack in the ceiling.

"Hello, my old son, fancy seeing you here!"
Mike turned around to see his friend Ian, with his trademark, half-smile, leaning against the wall.

"Ian? I've seen it all now. Why aren't you at the pub, you're usually there on days with a 'y' in them?"

"Very funny! I seem to recall you were no lightweight yourself back in the day, my friend! Anyway, the last thing I can remember was feeling a bit faint while I was walking up to the bar to get a round in ... Either I've died or this is a particularly unusual hangover."

"Do you have a headache?"

"No, actually. I feel at peace, almost sober! I need to go now, but I might see you later for a mineral water or something, if you're around?"

"Sounds good .. "

In an instant Ian had gone, but almost immediately a hospital scene was unfolding before Mike. A sombre-looking surgeon was talking to a lady whose face was obscured. The man exuded a calm air of gentle assurance as he spoke:

"Mrs   Reynolds, the aortic dissection operation   to   rebuild the blood vessel with a synthetic graft is always very difficult ... I'm afraid to tell you that your husband didn't come through the procedure. I am so very sorry."

Mike was stunned. The man faded away in the rapidly melting darkness, and Leanne's face came into view. She was standing right in front of him, crying but also endeavouring to smile.

"Please try not to worry about me, Mike, it's time for you to complete your journey now. I will join you when the time is right."

The man was no longer able to speak. Leanne was already slipping away from him, disappearing in the intense light; Mike needed to shield his eyes to catch a final glimpse of her. He heard her last words:

"I'll see you again soon, my love, we're never really apart. Just do me one favour: Go back for my dad, take him with you, I think he's ready now."

**

"Honesty must be the best policy, but it's important to remember that apparently, by elimination, dishonesty is the second best policy." -George Carlin

Back in the days
of Tanners and Bobs

By David Filmer

When Mothers had patience and Fathers had jobs.
When football team families wore hand me down shoes,
And T.V gave only two channels to choose.
Back in the days of three penny bits,
when schools employed nurses to search for your nits.
When snowballs were harmless; ice slides were permitted
and all of your jumpers were warm and hand knitted.
Back in the days of hot ginger beers,
when children remained so for more than six years.
When children respected what older folks said,
and pot was a thing you kept under your bed.
Back in the days of Listen with Mother,
when neighbours were friendly and talked to each other.
When cars were so rare you could play in the street.
When Doctors made house calls and Police walked the beat.
Back in the days of Milligan's Goons,
when butter was butter and songs all had tunes.
It was dumplings for dinner and trifle for tea,
and your annual break was a day by the sea.
Back in the days of Dixon's Dock Green,
Crackerjack pens and Lyons ice cream.
When children could freely wear National Health glasses,
and teachers all stood at the FRONT of their classes.
Back in the days of rocking and reeling,
when mobiles were things that you hung from the ceiling. When
woodwork and pottery got taught in schools,
and everyone dreamed of a win on the pools.
Back in the days when I was a lad,
I can't help but smile for the fun that I had.
Hopscotch and roller skates; snowballs to lob.
Back in the days of tanners and bobs.

Trick

Richard Seal

Jackie had always enjoyed cooking, particularly for people who liked to eat. Her late husband had loved his food, and ten year old son Toby was greatly appreciative of her imaginative culinary creations. His encouragement and positive feedback led her to attempt a wide range of dishes, from Duck a L'orange to Boeuf Bourguignon, and Black Forest Gateaux to baked Alaska.

On this particular Halloween Jackie was busy baking herself an extra-special birthday cake - she had mixed feelings about the prospect of turning forty the following week, but knew that her friends would be rallying around with banter and several bottles of wine to help her to keep such things in perspective. She had also decided that it would be the right time to stop smoking again - third time lucky she hoped.

At around eight o'clock she heard knocking on the door. Assuming that it would be her son, she wiped her hands on her apron and opened the door with a broad smile.

"Toby, darling, you could have used your key ... "

Four little children were standing in front of her, disguised in lurid, gruesome Halloween costumes, and giggling amongst themselves. "Trick or treat?"

She feigned shock and raised her hands to cover her face for a moment "Hi kids .. Or should I say little monsters? Wait just a minute, I've got some sweets here."

When she returned with a big bag of assorted candies, each of the children took turns to dig deep and take a large handful.

"Come on now, don't take too many, I don't have an endless supply you know." She frowned when she saw that the bag had been emptied before the fourth child had had his turn.

"Thanks lady! Happy Halloween! The first three children ran off leaving the last one, the smallest, standing there alone.

"I'm sorry, my love, I don't have any more. Run after your friends and make them share some of theirs with you."

The figure stood in silence for a few moments before repeating "Trick or treat?" in a curious, flat tone.

Jackie attempted a smile, but it was difficult to hide her irritation. She wanted to get back to her cake.

"Look, really, I have no more treats to give you. Go on, off you go now - catch up with your friends, I'm sure you'll get some more sweets at the next house."

After a pause he repeated his mantra again: "Trick or treat?"

"I've had enough now, dear, now I'm closing the door." Having left the child she returned to the kitchen but found that she could no longer focus on her baking. After about ten minutes, and still feeling slightly unsettled, she returned to the front door. When she opened it she was shocked to see that the diminutive figure was still standing there.

"Trick or treat?" The tone now sounded dead.

Jackie's heart flipped and she gasped as she took an involuntary step backwards. "Go away! I won't tell you again. There are no more treats, so I'll have to choose 'trick' - do your worst!"

She slammed the door, barely able to catch her breath. The shaken woman retreated to the living room to try to calm down, with the aid of a large glass of whisky and a couple of cigarettes.

Toby got home twenty minutes later. When he let himself in, he was surprised to see his mother sitting on the sofa, staring into space. "Are you okay Mum? You look pale. Aren't you giving up smoking?"

She tried to shake herself back to normality and forced herself to get to her feet. "Hello love, did you have a nice time with your friends tonight?"

"Yes, we had some pizza and played video games. It was fun." He looked around the room, then in the direction of the kitchen "I thought you were making your cake tonight?"

She looked at him, and swallowed hard, before speaking. "Yes, I'm working on it. Toby, do you know if any of your classmates were planning to go out 'Trick or Treating' tonight?"

"Yes, three of the boys said they were going to try to get as many treats as possible from the streets around this area. Have they already been round here?"

"Well, we had four visitors, actually. They cleaned me right out of sweets."

"Maybe it was a different group. These three kids do everything together, I can't imagine them bringing anyone else along for the ride."

"The other child was smaller, he stood slightly away from the others. Three of them took everything I had, left their friend with nothing ... "

"That certainly sounds like those three. I'll ask at school tomorrow to see if they took a fourth person tonight, but I would be surprised."

"Thanks, love. This little boy was strange, very quiet, he creeped me out to be honest."

"Okay, Mum, don't let it get to you. Halloween costumes can be pretty sick these days."

"We were happy with a pumpkin and candle when I was a girl." She grinned at him.

"I didn't realise they had pumpkins during the war .. " Toby ran off laughing as his Mum, who was laughing, aimed an exaggerated swipe in his direction.

Jackie did not sleep well that night. As she lay wide awake in the early hours she could hear their cat Freddie meowing loudly downstairs. Eventually the sound turned into a kind of wail and was accompanied by a frantic scratching. The woman sat bolt upright in bed - she remembered that they had had a cat flap fitted just two weeks ago to ensure that puss would be able to come and go as he pleased.

She considered waking her son, then decided against it. Jackie could feel the fear rising through her body as she walked slowly down the stairs.

"Freddie? Is that you? What's wrong my angel, are you hungry?"

She could hear nothing, but when she switched on the living room light there were traces of blood on the floor and the distinctive Halloween figure, still in costume, was standing in the middle of the room.

"Trick or treat?"

Jackie wasn't sure when the screaming was stopped by her having fainted, but the next thing she knew she was opening her eyes while lying on the floor, with her anxious son kneeling beside her.

"Are you alright now, Mum? You must have had a really bad nightmare or something. Have you been sleepwalking before?"

"Where's that boy? He was here, standing where you are now. And there was blood on the floor!" Jackie clutched Toby's arm, painfully catching the skin.

"There's no one here now, and I can't see any blood either .."

"I heard Freddie crying .. and he was scratching too .. Where is he?"

"Don't worry, you know how he likes to stay out all night sometimes, and it's not turned too cold yet. Maybe he brought a little mouse or bird in as a special birthday gift for you, then changed his mind and took it away. Come on, let's go back to bed."

The next morning Jackie felt much brighter and was wondering if she might have imagined the events of the previous evening. After taking Toby to school she enjoyed taking her time putting the finishing touches to her cake, then sat down to watch some afternoon TV with a strong coffee. After a while she began to feel drowsy so decided to have a little nap to catch up on some of her lost sleep. After a couple of hours she stirred when hearing something downstairs. She could not be sure if she had left the TV on, or perhaps Toby was home early from school.

Jackie yawned as she walked into the living room. The TV was off and everything was quiet in there. However, she could hear movements coming from the kitchen, it sounded a bit like an animal. Perhaps Freddie was home at last and something had followed him in through the flap. As she entered the room she stopped dead on seeing the Halloween figure again. He was vigorously working its way through her cake like a ravenous dog, grabbing hunks at a time. It stopped and turned to face her:

"Trick or treat ... ?"

Neighbour Karen let herself in with the key that Jackie had given her to use in emergencies. She had been alarmed by the sound of distress coming through the wall and came round immediately. She found a woman frozen to the spot in fear, pointing with a crooked finger.

"It was here again, the thing was eating my cake!"

"Who, Jackie? There's no one in here now." There was no sign of a person, a cake or anything out of the ordinary.

"That horrible creature from last night. It's playing nasty tricks on me to get its revenge. My Freddie has gone too!"

"Relax, there's nothing to be afraid of. I'm sure Freddie will be back when he starts getting hungry, like all males! I'm going to stay with you now and Toby will be home soon. I'll make us both a nice cup of tea."

When Toby got back, he and Karen took his mother, who seemed almost beyond speech, up to bed and then they returned to the living room.

"I'm a bit worried, Karen, Mum was very upset when I got home last night. She had seen something earlier and it really freaked her out."

"Has she been stressed lately, doing too much perhaps, feeling under a lot of strain?"

"I don't think so. She's been looking forward to celebrating her birthday, and has invited all her friends to a house party. She started making a cake last night when some kids came around doing 'Trick or Treat' and they gave her a fright or something."

"I don't like the practice either to be honest, the grisly costumes scare me a bit."

"I know what you mean. Mum kept talking about four boys calling round - But I know that there were only three of them, because they told me at school today that they were here last night. There was no fourth person ... "

"Let's stay down here for a while then we can go up and check on her. She'll probably feel better after a good sleep."

"I hope so ..."

Jackie was starting to feel that the line between being awake and living through a terrifying nightmare was becoming increasingly blurred. She had her eyes closed and lay perfectly still, focusing on her breath. Just as she was wondering again where Freddie might have gone she felt a weight at the end of the bed, pressing down on her feet.

She smiled and reached out her hand expecting to feel her beloved cat's fur. "Freddie, you're here at last .. Where have you .. "

The sensation of touching coarse fabric made Jackie open her eyes immediately. The dreaded figure was sitting silently on the bed. Battling to control her senses, the woman hissed at it:

"What do you want from me, you little freak? Are you trying to drive me mad?"

Before it could reply, Jackie cried out: "Let's see who's hiding behind this stupid costume!" As she tried to pull off the ghoul face she realised with terror that it was not a mask.

The thing's features shifted into a twisted leer before it exclaimed "Trick!" Flecks of its spittle landed on the woman's cheek.

Jackie was not aware that the bedroom door had just been opened as she reached under the bed and grabbed the baseball bat that she kept there in case she ever needed to ward off intruders. In a blind rage she lunged wildly at the creature and felt a sense of gratification at having made a heavy connection with its head. The resulting sound was a sickening combination of wet splat and splintering crack as blood and bone fragments spattered up the wall.

Karen reeled back and dropped to her knees in hysterical tears at having witnessed her dear friend and neighbour splitting her own son's skull open with devastating effectiveness and obvious glee.

**

"To be nobody but yourself in a world which is doing its best day and night to make you like everybody else means to fight the hardest battle which any human being can fight and never stop fighting." — E.E. Cummings

The Last Day (4)

Sarah Dawkins

I felt so alone
Thought I was wrong
Time stood still
I was ill
Nowhere to go
I didn't know
What to do
Feeling blue
It's my last day
Feeling this way

Out walking
Now talking
Turning it around
Now I have found
Life is much better
I am not bitter
Gratitude abounds
Abundance all around
A life full of love
Happiness thereof.

Pandora

Richard Seal

The middle-aged man walked down the long corridor of the draughty, cavernous house, with his long arms stretched behind his back, whistling under his breath and enjoying the sound of his heavy shoes on the polished wooden floors. Max then spent half an hour gazing out of a window at the vast grounds, watching the aged hedgerows, trees and bushes valiantly managing to remain erect in the face of strong winds and blustery November rain.

On hearing stirring from the floor above, the man strode across to the great staircase; he straightened his tie, adjusted his waistcoat and stared accusingly at his pocket watch. He listened to the familiar shuffling footsteps approaching painfully slowly. As the very old lady finally reached the bottom of the stairs, looking a little unsteady on her feet, Max kissed her lightly on the cheek and gently guided her to a nearby chair.

"Rest, awhile, Nanny, you need to preserve your strength. The winter is pervasive, and it is starting to take a hold of your soul."

"Hush, child. The weight of time is inexorably descending upon one and all. However, we don't need to admit aloud that it is laying us low."

"Indeed, one's counsel needs to be kept."

"Come. I will take tea now, Max, walk with me."

He helped her to her feet, and supported her arm as they made their way together towards the drawing room. "Tea taken at four o'clock is a custom which will not be thwarted, Nanny, I trust you believe that this will always be so."

As they took their refreshments in a tranquil silence, Max scrutinised his cucumber sandwich with avid curiosity, then leaned in close to the ornate silver stand as if about to confide in one of Nanny's fairy cakes. The woman shot him a sideways glance as she lifted the pot to refill their china cups.

"Speak, child, I feel that your heart needs to be unburdened, an air of anxiety is permeating the dying embers of the day."

"Nanny, we need to be protected from unwelcome forces." The man looked thoughtful.

"Explain yourself further. We live many miles from the nearest habitation, and visitors to the Hall are seldom received, and have, of course, never been welcome. Vital supplies are necessary on occasion, of course, and the delivery service that we utilise is satisfactorily discreet."

"I am in accordance with this assessment of the situation, save for one key omission. Time must not be permitted to cross the threshold, and should be vigorously resisted. Its ravages must desist forthwith."

"Do I take it, Max, that you have in mind the notion of conjuring up another creation? This is a grave and dangerous development, I fear no good can ever come of your black powers."

"You refer, of course, to the unfortunate incident with Ivan. I admit to being misguided in my attempts to create a perfect childhood companion, but at that time I was but a naive and callow youth."

"Max, the creature of your imagination was a vile abomination. The actions that were required to terminate its existence were heinous and have left the perpetrators diminished."

"The necessary decisive measures were taken by us, Nanny, and full responsibility has been accepted. We endure, and rest assured that my solution on this occasion is designed to ensure our ultimate strengthening."

"Share your thoughts with me, Max. It has always been the way that you have been able to lighten your load."

"I will create a bespoke animal, so much more than a mere pet, it is going to be a fiercely strong and imposing beast which will display aggression to any outsiders yet great affection and loyalty to ourselves. Nothing will pass without our expressed permission."

"How, pray, will you ensure that evil does not play a part in this process? I fear that we have been rendered by fading flames and will be unable to incinerate an undesirable a second time."

"Fear not, I will ensure that only reputable dog breeds are summoned to be included in the mix. There will be the strength and primal aspects of the Rottweiler, Doberman and Bull Terrier, tempered by the nature of the Labrador and Sheepdog."

"Have you fully thought this through, given the matter your most considered attention, Max?"

"The decision has been taken. I will retire below after sunset to begin work."

Early the next morning Nanny was making her way towards the bathroom when she heard a loud panting and heavy footfall behind her. She turned to see Max with an enormous imposing creature, which had the appearance of a wild dog, restrained by a thick rope.

"Nanny, allow me to introduce Pandora. She will ensure nothing unwelcome can reach us within these walls." The man paused, seeing the old lady's perplexed expression. "You have a doubt?"

"The animal looks untamed, unquiet?"

"My commands will be obeyed. Aspects of the wolf were included, I admit, but within reasonable parameters. Watch."

Max removed the tether and the 'dog' scrutinised the humans for a moment, before turning away from them and sitting down to groom herself.

"Pandora will be docile with us at all times, but this behaviour will not be replicated in the face of any external threat."

The 'dog' started to walk away, and showed no signs of stopping despite the man's demands for her to stay. "Fear not, the obedience training will start presently."

Nanny watched the creature come to a halt a short distance away; she licked a paw and then fixed them with an inscrutable look before settling into a low growl. "An aspect leaves me uneasy, Max, tell me more about our new companion?"

"I had an inspired notion. To ensure that our protector would have intelligence, independence, cunning and sharp instinct I decided to give her the brain of a cat ... "

"A cat? Child, what have you done?"

Max turned to see Pandora approaching them with slow, deliberate steps, tail fluffed out, claws visible, pupils narrowed, and huge teeth bared. The sound that she was emitting was far more sinister than that made by any dog. Resistance was futile.

**

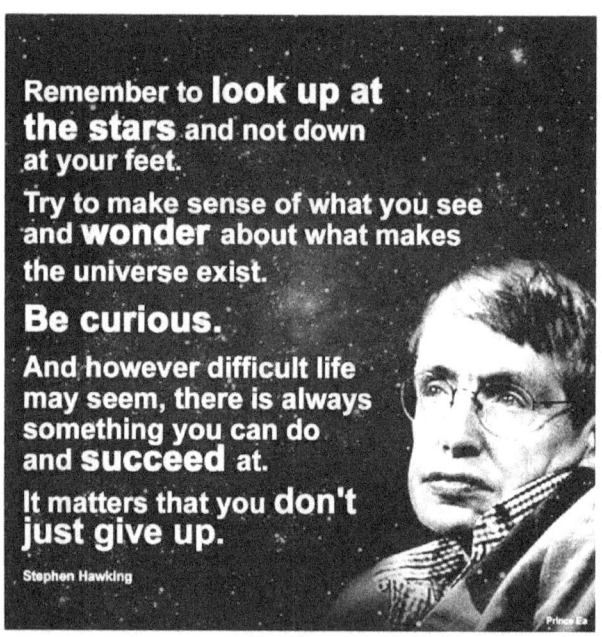

Charleston

Told by Richard Seal
"Bloomsbury paints in circles, lives in squares, and loves in triangles." - Dorothy Parker

The Bloomsbury painters, Vanessa Bell, Duncan Grant, and Roger Fry, are regarded as significant contributors to the new movements in British art in the early twentieth century. Their painting is domestic and rich with sensuous beauty. French Post-Impressionism touched their art, while the influence of Mediterranean culture can be seen in the colours and patterns of walls, ceramics and furniture decorations.

In 1916, on writer Virginia Woolf's recommendation, Vanessa (Woolf's sister) and Duncan, his friend and lover David Garnett, and Vanessa's two sons, Julian aged eight and Quentin aged six, moved to Charleston farmhouse in East Sussex. Dating from the late sixteenth century and altered in the nineteenth century, it was to be occupied and brought to life by the family and their friends for the next sixty-four years. Almost from the start, the artists began to decorate the house. This artwork, and the accumulation of paintings, furnishings and other objects, continued throughout their lives. The garden was also developed under Fry's guidance.

Vanessa had previously stayed at Little Talland House in Firle, and at nearby Asheham House which Virginia and Leonard Woolf still leased. Clive Bell, whose marriage to Vanessa had by this time drifted into a friendship, spent the war years doing farm work at Garsington Manor in Oxfordshire. Grant and Garnett, as conscientious objectors, needed to find 'work of national importance' on a farm or face the prospect of going to prison. Charleston was in an ideal location, in an area that the artists knew and which had the relative seclusion that would enable them to continue exploring intense, unconventional, artistic lifestyles.

Charleston provided a country retreat for this group of artists, writers and intellectuals who became known collectively as 'Bloomsbury'. Many of them had met around the turn of the century as students at Cambridge University. They gathered from 1904 in the Bloomsbury district of London, at the home of Vanessa, Thoby, Virginia and Adrian Stephen. Vanessa wrote of that time: 'We did not hesitate to talk of anything … you could say what you liked about art, sex and religion'. These conversations were to continue at Charleston during the war years.

'The group were interested in working out a new way of living here, a different approach to friendships, relationships and family life,' says Megan Wright, of the Charleston Trust.

'And so the many changing physical relationships within the group weren't ever in the closet for them – not so much a source of scandal – and not as important as the enduring friendships they shared.' Julian and Quentin grew up in an atmosphere of freedom, roaming the downs, sailing boats on the pond and digging in the mud. At the house, on Christmas Day 1918, Vanessa gave birth to Angelica, her

daughter by Duncan. Years later, David Garnett and
Angelica were to marry, as he had predicted.

Despite the discomforts – there was no hot water, and the
house was very cold – there were always a large number of
guests. Clive Bell, sometimes with companion Mary
Hutchinson, attended regularly as did Roger Fry, organiser
of the Post-Impressionist exhibitions of 1910 and 1912, and
founder of the Omega Workshops in 1913. Economist John
Maynard Keynes came so often that he was given his own
room in which he wrote his book 'The Economic
Consequences of the Peace' (1919). Alongside Virginia and
Leonard Woolf, other visitors over the years included
writers T. S. Eliot and E. M. Forster, essayist Lytton
Strachey, and Desmond and Molly MacCarthy.

During the inter-war years the house was largely used by the
family as a holiday home, a period which was later
described by Quentin as 'the golden age of Charleston'.
However, the peace and tranquillity was shattered in 1937
when Vanessa received the devastating news that her elder
son Julian had been killed in the Spanish Civil War; plagued
by depression, Virginia took her own life four years later.
When the Second World War broke out in 1939, Vanessa,
Duncan and Clive Bell decided to move to Charleston
permanently.

Vanessa died in 1961, Clive in 1964. Duncan continued to
live at Charleston until just before his death, aged ninetry
three, in 1978. Angelica moved in to the house and lived
there alone until 1980, when The Charleston Trust was
formed. Today the house appears as it was in the 1950s,

representing a way of life in which beautiful surroundings, and works of art were of primary importance. It is a living artwork with its ceramics, textiles, colourful furniture and paintings. Charleston has become, as Quentin wrote, 'a kind of time capsule in which the public can examine a world which has vanished'.

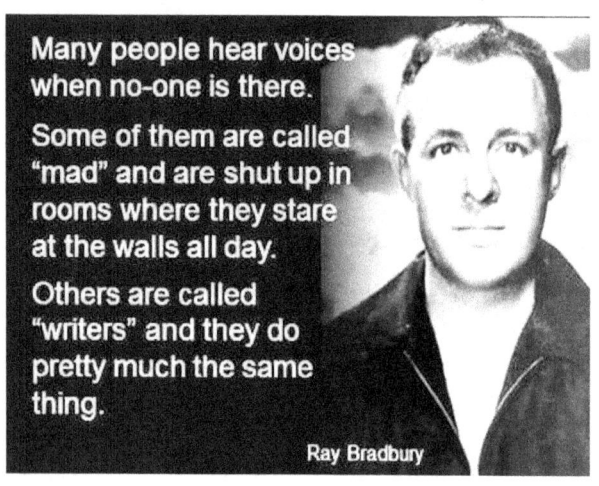

Many people hear voices when no-one is there.

Some of them are called "mad" and are shut up in rooms where they stare at the walls all day.

Others are called "writers" and they do pretty much the same thing.

Ray Bradbury

**

Half an hour before the start of the morning, an employee calls his supervisor to say he won't be coming in today.
Employee: "I'm having a vision problem."
Supervisor: "Sounds bad. What's wrong?"
Employee: "I just can't see myself at work today."

Smile

Sarah Dawkins

Smile for a while
Improve your lifestyle
Bring kindness in
Produce a grin
Light up your face
Slow down your pace
Relax and unwind
Your soul you may find
Be still and listen
Inside is hidden
A message for you
When you're feeling blue
Your soul will speak
Pictures may creep
Into your mind
Become aligned
And what you see
Just let it be
Notice the feeling
Start your healing

Granny's Garden Seat

Richard Seal

Granny's garden had always been her pride and joy. From rose bushes to rhododendron, the woman knew how everything grew - she was aware of the fragrant power of every flower. Leading visitors on a tour of her garden, unbridled joy would guide her walk, spilling over into her talk, with blooming treasures discovered every day on this precious ground. She dressed all of her hanging baskets gaily, and tended them daily.

Just before Easter, Granny had led her fifteen year old granddaughter Emily to the very end of the garden, and showed her an opening at which she had not noticed before at the side of the privet hedge. This led to a stone seat, almost completely obscured by foliage and shrouded in shadows. The lady beamed at its sight, and took the teenager's hand:

"This is such a special place for me, Emily, it holds so many happy memories."

"Did you come and sit here a lot, Gran?"

"Oh yes, I loved looking after the plants - of course! - and playing with my little sister. But I would always retreat to this area to be on my own, perhaps to read or draw a little, but mostly just to reflect on life. Ask your mother, she used to come here too, especially when she was your age."

"It must have been relaxing."

"Yes, such a welcome break from the noise of life. You can come here any time of course, even though you don't have siblings to escape from. Your mum would never let her younger sisters join her. The strange thing is that they had no real interest, and neither did my sister who just wanted to run and play all the time."

"Do you mind if I stay for a while?"

Granny patted her arm. "Of course, my dear, I would be delighted if you would. I'm going back inside now, take your time and enjoy the peace."

Emily moved some of the fronds of ivy aside and sat down. She closed her eyes for a few minutes, listening to her own heartbeat and imagining what it must have been like for Mum and Granny doing the same thing so many years ago. As she felt herself drifting away, a ball of light and warmth began to expand in her consciousness ... the spell was only broken by the unwelcome sound of a message arriving on her mobile phone. Unable to resist the urge to ignore the intrusion, she checked her messages, and was puzzled to have received a video attachment entitled 'Play me, 1958". She was so intrigued by the title that she opened it without hesitation.

The short black-and-white film started with footage of a slim, dark-haired teenager kneeling on the lawn tending to the flower beds. She looked totally absorbed in what she was doing, with her gloveless fingers probing the soil. Suddenly another girl walked into the shot. She looked a couple of years younger, and was giggling as she pushed the older one forward into the plants. As the victim turned around, Emily could recognise her Gran from old photographs. The dialogue was only just audible:

"Sorry, Annie, I just couldn't resist doing that."

Her sister looked annoyed, but half-amused too: "That's okay, I can't resist doing this either!" Annie aimed a slap in the younger girl's direction, but missed. She chased her out of the frame, both of them laughing.

After a brief fade the movie resumed with Annie and her sister taking photographs of each other. Then the action switched to the older girl walking to the bottom of the garden, looking over her shoulder, then disappearing behind the hedge. In the shady sanctuary the girl held up a photograph album containing a picture of herself and nothing else. She slipped the book into a hole beneath the stone seat, then turned to the camera, put her finger to her lips and the screen went black ...

Before Emily had the chance to go take a look beneath her seat, another video arrived on her phone, this time entitled 'Play Me, 1988' .. The film was in colour this time. Granny, now an adult in her forties, was strolling around the garden with a blond teenage girl, who she instantly recognised as her mother, Sally, while Gran was showing her various flowers and shrubs, the teenager was struggling to conceal her boredom. She yawned at one point then rolled her eyes, which invoked her mother's irritation.

"Okay, I get the message that you're not interested! Now, Sally, I'm going to take your photograph whether you like it or not. Give me a big smile please, it won't hurt you to look cheerful."

The girl muttered something inaudible but relaxed her pout long enough for Gran to capture a satisfactory shot. "Is that okay, can I go now?"

"Of course, go and wash your hands ready for tea"

The next scene showed the teenager in the secret area. She was wearing headphones, and it looked like she was singing to herself. Sally could be seen slipping something into the album, before returning it to the hiding place. Finally, the girl looked directly at the camera and blew a kiss ...

Emily sat very still for a few moments, before tentatively lifting the flat stone to investigate ... The photograph album was still there, with in containing smiling pictures of both Gran and Mum, taken three decades apart. There were only three pages, and she knew it was her turn to join the party.

She took short video and a photo of herself, then returned to the house, printed the picture, and added it to the book.

Two days later Granny was found dead in her garden. It was almost as if she had chosen the exact moment to pass away in her bed of daffodils, knowing that her tulips would be returning soon. A couple of months later, the house was sold to a builder. .

Returning to the house with her mother for the final time, Emily felt melancholy as she imagined the man casually tossing things into a skip. However, she felt amused at the thought that once the builder set foot outside extreme caution would be required - if Gran's baskets were allowed to overflow with weeds, or her blooms were neglected, she would bring dire retribution down on his head. The teenager found, to her horror, that the album was not there. On the verge of tears, she ran into the house.

"What's the matter, Emily? I've got a lot of sorting to do and we haven't got long."

"The old photograph album under the seat in the garden, it's gone!"

"What are you talking about, love, what photograph ..." She stopped in mid-sentence. "The album ... I haven't thought about that for years ... When I was about your age, Granny insisted that I include a picture of myself next to one of her, I thought it was so silly at the time."

"There were photographs of three generations inside. And now it's gone." Sally looked at her daughter. "You added your picture? When?"

"Just before Gran died, can I tell you the full story?" . . .

It was getting late by the time everything was finished. Mother and daughter decided to pay a final visit to the garden. There was still no sign of the book, and they sat in silent reflection in the dying light for ten minutes. Sally spoke first.

"Come on Em, we need to make a move. This is only a house and garden, the memories will stay with us always." Emily nodded. "Can I stay here for just a couple more minutes, Mum?"

"Of course, I'll get the car ready."

As her mother walked away, Emily received 'Play Me, 2018'. She watched the brief film of herself before an attachment entitled 'Always' came through. For a moment a recent image of Granny appeared; she winked at the teenager, before her face dissolved into a photograph of the three teenagers, beaming, sitting beside each other on the stone seat.

**

Champagne

Richard Seal

The middle aged man pauses in front of the sliding glass doors before entering the building for the first time in thirty years. The decades seem to have diminished his supermarket, almost beyond recognition. These tight aisles once seemed like vast thoroughfares, and the plentiful staff have now been stripped down to a few bored-looking youths. He approaches the fruit and vegetables section with butterflies and considerable trepidation ...

The Supermarket job gave this lad a new lease of life. This young assistant shook off a sixteen year old's shyness, and the shuffling blushing through the pain of a day at school, to enjoy Saturdays strolling, sometimes prowling, around aisles of fruit and vegetables. He carried potato sacks with panache, handling lemons with calm authority, so coolly rearranging his cabbages. At the end of each shift he felt a surge of power when wielding the pricing gun, free to reduce whatever took his fancy. He often hovered awhile tantalising little groups of lurking chancers all waiting to grab his bags of bargain bananas or knock-down nectarines.

After a few weeks the lad had reinvented his introversion by smiling at the quiet girl across the aisle before looking away in flushes. He had felt overwhelmed at the first staff Christmas party, losing focus and inhibitions after mixing his drinks with his section mates, before slipping away to steal a fleeting kiss with his favourite girl in the cloakroom before her Dad arrived early to take her home. The evening, already in a whirl, ended with him winning a huge bottle of champagne in the raffle. He resisted those urging him to crack the bottle open as he was so thrilled about saving it for a special festive gift for his Mum.

... His old section is now half the size, unstaffed, the produce looks neglected, unloved. He wonders whether wackiness still to be found in the warehouse, laughter heard in the loading bay. One assistant looks like the girl he will never forget; much older of course, and a little tireder. She holds his gaze for a moment, smiling slightly, before looking down then away into the jams and preserves.

**

When in Spain

Christopher Wyatt

There is a little restaurant, Far, far away
Where the menu's all in Spanish (that's an easy thing you say)
Beware the wording though it's not what we have here,
I read the line, one word I saw, Aha, I thought, I know that dish
And read it to the waiter as being what I wish.
But when it came oh what a shock
I thought I'd seen it all
But the meal that graced my dish I'd never seen before.
I looked at it, it looked at me whatever shall I do?
Sod it I thought and ate the lot and had no cause to rue.
'Cause when your starved you'll eat what's given even if its cr.p. The moral being, learn the lingo, don't fall in the trap,
You think you know but if you don't by then it's far too late,
You may end up, just as I did, with weird things on your plate.

Animal Whisperer

Richard Seal

The eldest of three sisters, Sue embraces a hectic life which keeps her much too busy; she relishes rushing around amid her ever-expanding brood, and is more than happy to adopt the role of harassed mother hen. An indeterminate number of stray cats, two large dogs, and three rabbits sit alongside the woman's husband and daughter under her protective wing. She keeps her head down and steadfastly refuses to contemplate the grim prospect of ever being faced with an empty nest.

Middle sister Jenny's heart is full of compassion for animals, especially dogs. Her beloved Rottweiler Abigail is her whole world. Despite the fact that her previous fur babies, Hannah and Eva, were taken from her much too soon, they continue to provide the woman with inner strength, comfort and succour. All the precious girls, whether still alive or having already passed, gather with infectious joy around her feet, providing invaluable protection from encroaching doubts and fears.

Youngest sister Maggie's face always fills with ecstasy at the sight of animals, her smile wider than that of the Cheshire Cat. In photographs taken from the ages of four to forty she has been adorned by an assortment of feline friends. While passing dogs are casually ruffled, birds chirruped at, and guinea pigs given special belly tickles, a puss is always at the top of the woman's list. She speaks to them in excited, secret whispers, luxuriating in each ear twitch, and delighting in paw gyrations.

Watching the three middle-aged ladies chatting to each other in animated fashion over tea and cakes on Sunday afternoons, Maggie's portly cat pauses for a spell of paw-cleaning and a leisurely yawn. Monty takes a little step backwards, his eyes narrow, nose twitches, thick ginger fur ripples and his tail flicks, before he silently slinks away to find himself a sun spot.

**

Bus Tour

Groups of Americans were traveling by tour bus through Holland.

As they stopped at a cheese farm, a young guide led them through the process of cheese making, explaining that goat's milk was used. She showed the group a lovely hillside where many goats were grazing. 'These' she explained, 'Are the older goats they are put out to pasture when they no longer produce.'

She then asked, 'What do you do in America with your old goats?'

A spry old gentleman answered, 'They send us on bus tours!

**

A government which robs Peter to pay Paul can always depend on the support of Paul.
George Bernard Shaw

Buried

Richard Seal

Mike can feel himself slipping further and further down under the weight of a collapsing marriage, the spectre of impending redundancy, huge mortgage payments, the loan for his new car, and the kids' exorbitant school fees. Living well beyond his means has sunk him into a pit, he is slowly being buried alive. Each night, lying awake in bed for hours, the man feels burned out, wanting to shout, surrounded by dark clay ...

In sleep, he becomes weightless, timeless, drifting through space; now displaced without form or sense of alarm, moving beyond calm into a realm lacking thought. Then dim figures from the past mutate, degenerate into shade-faded creatures of hate, bringing naked fright in the very deepest dead of night. A flesh tremor sent down his spine feels so intense whilst he is lying prone, without any form of defence.

Concealed behind the curtains or under the bed, lingers a sickening dread, a fear of death, nothingness and beyond. A slight figure appears nightly as a streak. A grime-grey shroud of cloud dissipating into a dirty stain. Mike asks himself in fleeting moments of consciousness if this shadow lady huddled in the corner, pulling at her long grey hair, imploring, trying to scream, rising to fall, is actually there at all.

As a small black cat sidles underneath his bed, the darkness gathers around cobwebs to form a tiny figure in a shapeless hat; she hovers above the stricken man awhile; she could be kindly with a half smile, but falters a moment in black, green to grisly mean. Puss emerges in the fading night - his enigmatic magic is, for now, dissipated by scant daylight.

Heavy rain and a loud branch crack end the nightmares, but not the interminable feeling of blackness. The morning returns him to the daytime show awhile. A range of roles to be performed with diligence, vigour; each of his faces are different, shifting, and always presented with a valiant smile. Mike knows only too well that the next night will attack, change tack, bringing many different realities back

... Submerged, going under, soil sputtering in his mouth, heavy cold-sweating, limbs like lead, he is yearning now for the last spadeful to be thrown over his head.

Just Smile that Happy Smile

Caroline Goss

When you smile it just makes you feel so happy,
Not sad or mad, or bad and snappy!

What things can you think of that make you smile?
Don't answer now, just wait a while.

Think of happy times with loved ones and friends,
Just let your mind wander and go where it wends.

Where is it taking you, to far and distant lands,
Or childhood memories of sun, sea and sand?

Those hazy, lazy days of a never ending summer,
I really hope it's not anything glummer!

Or meeting up after time apart,
Of a long lost friend, where do you start!

That special hug, that long lingering kiss,
Those happy days they seemed such bliss.

Your baby's first cry at the time of its birth
How joyous you feel as it enters this earth.

Or future events that are about to occur,
OK, OK! It's a bit of a blur!

Let's go to the present and that time is now,
Are you smiling or don't you know how?

Just think of something that makes you happy,
Not sad or mad, or bad and snappy!

Meg

(Not our Host!)

Trudie Oakley

It was no good; Meg just couldn't sleep. The air conditioning was humming quietly and successfully keeping the moist tropical heat at bay, but it wasn't the heat that was the reason for her restlessness.

Just a few days ago her dear Ben had surprised her by proposing and presenting her with a most beautiful ring, and just to make things perfect he had whisked her away for a week to this beautiful five star hotel, but things were not perfect.

She crept stealthily from the bedroom and threw on a flimsy dress before stepping out into the sultry night. A gate at the rear of the hotel lead directly onto a private beach which was now deserted and the only sound she could hear was that of the ocean lapping gently onto the sand. She walked along the waters' edge grateful for the caress of the cooling water on her feet.

She thought of Harry and felt the inevitable trickle of tears that always accompanied the constant ache that she felt without him. She'd adored Harry almost from the first time she had laid eyes on him and the two years they had enjoyed together before he was killed were the happiest she had ever known, but giving your heart to a serving soldier was a very risky business and she had learnt that in the very hardest way.

Three years after losing Harry she had been introduced to Ben by a mutual friend and they had immediately recognised in each other a kindred spirit and almost inevitably had grown closer and now, just one year later here she was alone wrestling with her conscience. Just a few weeks ago her mother, who probably understood Meg better than she did herself, had asked what was wrong, and without too much prompting Meg had admitted that Harry was still in her heart and although she loved Ben it was not in the overwhelming way that made her want to spend the rest of her life with him. Her mother had held her just as she had when a child and said she knew that Meg would do the right thing by Ben; if she really could not love him in the right way it was only fair to be honest and let him get on with the rest of his life.

Meg turned back toward the hotel entrance watching the reflection of the lamp lights ripple on the dark smooth water and disappearing into nothingness. She crept back into their room and stood watching Ben sleep. He was so handsome and kind, she was going to hurt him so. She slipped off her ring and placed it on his bedside table turning away with tear filled eyes. She would spend the night on the terrace lounger. She just couldn't join him in bed now that she had made up her mind, it would be disloyal; he deserved better than that.

The slight breeze tousled her hair as she sat underneath a crescent moon wondering how on earth she could let Ben down lightly. She had been unfair to him letting things get this far and in her own way she loved him dearly and would do almost anything to avoid hurting him, but she had to do this for both their sakes.

She woke with Ben standing over her, ring in hand. He helped her to her feet and they clung together. Eventually Meg found her voice, "I'm sorry Ben but it's just that…"

Ben placed a finger on her lips and shook his head "I understand Meg. I know – I suppose always known."

**

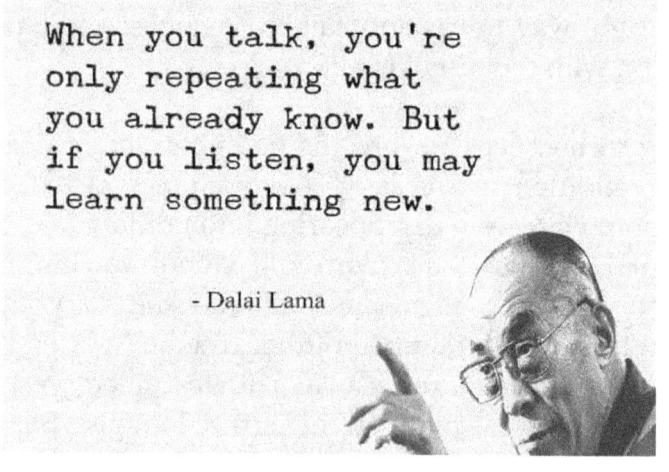

When you talk, you're only repeating what you already know. But if you listen, you may learn something new.

- Dalai Lama

Daisy Chain

Richard Seal

One day, decades ago, walking down this country lane, he had learned all about making daisy chains. A sunny girl had shot this boy her prettiest smile, inviting him to enter her front garden for a while. Sat together on the grass for barely ten minutes amid freckles, giggles, and thoughts of a kiss, their daisies were carefully selected, then linked into a chain which she had placed around his neck. He had left it there all day.

His thoughts drift towards the housing estate at the end of the lane, which long ago replaced the fields of childhood. He sees that only a couple of the hedges have survived. He can feel the thrill of the adrenaline rush returning with vivid memories of picking over a hundred blackberries, so large and luscious in their purple-black ripeness, on the walk home from school. As a rule his haul of berries was so much bigger than his siblings', and he had proudly hailed himself the co-creator of Mum's great blackberry pies.

However, stopping to look now at these barren bushes, he can feel the squashy fruit staining his fingers, some of the other berries are a hard, frigid green; thorns are jabbing his skin again and a cluster of wasps is poised, ready to move in for the kill. Suddenly he feels aware that the blackberries have been replaced in his adulthood by a tangled mass of brambles. The lawns are now perfectly manicured, some with stripes, and there is no sign of any clover, buttercups or daisies.

From the Soul of a Community Cat
I have no name, I have no home,
I'm not lost, just unloved and alone.
I hunt by day and seek warmth at night,
Only to awake to the emptiness of light.
I think, I feel, I love, I cry, and
Just like you, I'd rather live than die.
I pray to God you'll help give me a voice,
Being homeless and alone, was NOT by choice.

**

AN ELECTRIC COMPANY SIGN:
"We would be delighted if you send in your payment on time.   However, if you don't, YOU will be de-lighted."

Monkey

Richard Seal

When she was a child, Cathy's father used to tell her a story about an old busker who travelled around Birmingham on the bus with his monkey. She would often snuggle up to dad when he came home from his shift at the factory, smelling of oil and smoke, and ask for more details about this magical creature. The scanty facts that he was able to provide were enhanced by her vivid imagination, and the girl enjoyed fantasising about him

living with her instead - the two of them would have such fun and games together. She would wake up feeling happy and energised, even on a school day, whenever she had had a dream about him the previous night.

One day, the girl was sitting on the bus with her dad, when he suddenly nudged her in the ribs and whispered excitedly: "That's the man that I've been telling you about, and look - he's got his monkey companion with him."

Cathy sat frozen in her seat in rapt attention. Her blue eyes widened almost as quickly as her pulse rate was increasing. "The monkey! I can't believe he's real." Without further ado she leapt to her feet and went straight over to where the man was sitting. "Hello sir, how are you? Can I say 'hello' to your wonderful monkey? Please!"

The man looked up at her. He had a pale, heavily lined face and a hint of a glint in his dark brown eyes. He said nothing but gave her just the suggestion of a smile and he nodded his head slowly. Cathy clapped her hands rapidly in unbridled joy and put her hand on the creature's fur. It felt soft, warm and comforting like the rug in front of the log fire that their beloved cat Tinkle used to love.

The girl was intrigued by the fact that the monkey's arms, legs, and long tail were dark while the rest of his body was white. She thought the cap of black fur on top of his head was extra cute. "Hello, what's your name? It's lovely to meet you."

She made eye contact with the monkey and to her it seemed as if he was telling her that everything would be okay and there was no need to worry about anything. When it was time for the animal and his human friend to get off the bus, it was impossible for Cathy to feel sad because the creature turned his head to look back at her and he gave a reassuring wink as if to say that they would meet again soon.

As the weeks passed by the girl kept an eye out for her new friend around the town, but to no avail. The man no longer busked in his previous spot near the railway station, and Cathy was beginning to wonder if they might have moved to a different area when her father took her to one side one morning and broke the news to her that the man had sadly passed away.

"I'm sorry about the man, but what about the monkey? Where is he, what has happened to him?"

"I'm sorry, love, I don't know," he said, sadly.

"Please find out, Daddy, please! I need to see him again." She was weeping by this point, and her stilted words came between sobs.

Cathy felt a gnawing melancholy deep within as the weeks turned into months, and Daddy was unable to give her any updated information about the monkey. He said that her friend was probably in a happy place, somewhere where the sun shines a lot and there are places for animals to have fun, play and explore. However, his daughter remained unconvinced and hoped that the poor creature was not in distress and in desperate need of her help. She took no notice of her horrible aunt who had taken to telling her each time she came round that monkeys should not be kept as pets. The woman was clearly not sensitive enough to understand that there was much more to their relationship - they were soul mates, and their connection was something deep and spiritual.

Just before Christmas, the girl said her prayers and as usual the monkey was included in her thoughts. As she was about to drop off to sleep, she heard a rustling sound. When she opened her eyes she was thrilled to see that the monkey was sitting on the end of the bed.

"Hello, Cathy, how are you? Are you pleased to see me?" The animal exuded warmth.

She stared at the creature in disbelief. He was not actually speaking but she found that she could hear his thoughts somehow. "I'm so happy you're here, so relieved that you're alive."

"I'm with you, dear child. Everything is okay."

She reached out to hug him, but his physical form eluded her and her little hands flailed in the air. "I can't feel you, what's happened to your body? Are you dead like the old man?"

"Don't think about things like that, just remember that you don't have to feel anxious about anything. I will appear whenever you need me."

"Always be my friend?"

"I promise. Forever." His presence was so comforting.

As Cathy moved into her teenage years, she knew she always had her monkey to turn to. This thought helped her to overcome so many doubts and fears, she felt confident, happy and secure; unlike family and friends, he never changed, got older or moved on. Even though other people said that they could not see her dear friend, and she became very selective about who she talked to about him, she knew that he was there and that was all that mattered to them both. When the girl got a Saturday job working at a clothes shop at the age of sixteen, he would travel on the bus to keep her company on the journey to work.

One day Cathy spotted a little girl, with her father, sitting a few rows back, pointing excitedly in their direction. She knew that this child was special, a kindred spirit, so beckoned her over with the warmest smile that she could manage. She gave her a big hug. "Hello. What's your name?"

"I'm Emma, please can I play with your monkey?" The girl was overwhelmed by joy.

"Of course you can. My name is Cathy, by the way. Let me introduce you to our secret forever friend. He will never let us down."

The little girl's father and several of the other passengers looked puzzled to see the two girls crying and laughing at the same time.

**

Oliver Cromwell's Speech to the English Parliament 20th April, 1653.

Facebook: BRITISH MILITARY HUMOUR

It is high time for me to put an end to your sitting in this place, which you have dishonoured by your contempt of all virtue, and defiled by your practice of every vice; ye are a factious crew, and enemies to all good government; ye are a pack of mercenary wretches, and would like Esau sell your country for a mess of pottage, and like Judas betray your God for a few pieces of money.

Is there a single virtue now remaining amongst you? Is there one vice you do not possess? Ye have no more religion than my horse; gold is your God; which of you have not barter'd your consience for bribes? Is there a man that has the least care for the good of the Commonwealth? Ye sordid prostitutes, have you not defil'd this sacred place, and turned the Lord's temple into a den of thieves, by your immoral principles and picked practices? Ye are grown intolerably odious to the whole nation; you were deputed here by the people to get grievances redress'd, are yourselves gone!

So! Take away that shining bauble there, and lock up the doors. In the name of God, go!

Percychatteybooks

Story Telling (R)

Somerset House

6070 Birmingham Business Park

Birmingham

B37 7BF

Registered Number 2299335